Falling Star

By Charles Huss

I0547249

ISBN: 979-8-9886374-7-9

To my mom, Nancy, for being the perfect example of what a great mom should be and for helping me find errors in my text.

Chapter 1

"Shhh! Quiet!" Emma said, trying to hear over the crackling of the fire. "Do you hear that?"

Corinne and her boyfriend, Andy, sat on a log beside Emma. Corinne said, "I don't hear anything."

"Exactly," Emma said. "We've been on this trail for weeks. When was the last time you heard nothing? There's always something out there making noise. Suddenly, all the animals and insects are quiet."

They both looked around while straining to hear. "Weird," Andy said. "I wonder if they know something we don't."

"It's possible," Emma said. "Animals are much more in tune with nature than we are. Maybe something is going on that we don't know about. We should be extra cautious tonight."

"I think you worry too much, Emma," Corinne said. "A little quiet never hurt anyone."

"It's not the quiet that I'm worried about," Emma said. "It's what caused the quiet that worries me."

Corinne was about to say something, but was interrupted when a fireball streaked over their heads and crashed less than a half mile away. They saw a flash of light through the trees. A few seconds later, they heard a thunderous sound as the ground shook beneath their feet.

They all stood up and looked at the orange glow coming from the forest. "Holy Shit!" Andy said.

"A falling star," said Corrine.

"That was a meteorite."

"I know what it's called, Andy."

"Let's go check it out."

"I'm game," Corinne said. "What about you, Emma?"

"No, thank you," Emma said. "I have no desire to traipse through the woods in the middle of the night looking for some rock. It's too dangerous."

"It's not just a rock," Andy said. "It is a rock from outer space."

"Oh, come on, Emma. You can't always be the practical one," Corinne said. "You need to do something crazy every once in a while."

"I came on this hike with you two. That's crazy enough for me. You go ahead. I'll keep the fire going until you get back."

"Are you sure? I hate to leave you here alone."

"I'm sure. Go ahead. I'll be fine."

"Corinne looked at Andy and said, "She'll be fine. Let's go check it out."

They both grabbed a flashlight from their bags and headed into the forest. It was slow going without a trail to follow. In some places, the vegetation was too thick to get through, so they had to go out of their way to get around it. In the distance, they could see an orange glow. That was their beacon. They knew where they had to go.

They walked for almost thirty minutes. Most of the way was difficult, but they did encounter a small area without obstacles. When they got close enough, they saw several trees lying on their sides and an elongated rock about the size of a punching bag at the center of a crater that was at least ten feet wide. The rock was still so hot that it glowed orange.

"Wow! That is so cool," Andy said.

They walked to the crater's edge, and Andy said, "Did you ever see anything like that?"

"No," Corinne said. "This is so exciting. I feel like I'm on top of the world."

"I know what you mean," Andy said. "Don't you just want to scream?"

"Let's do it," Corinne said, and they both screamed at the top of their lungs."

Corinne checked her pockets and said, "I want to get a picture of it, but I left my phone in my bag. Do you have your phone?"

Andy checked his pockets. "No. Unfortunately, I left mine back at camp, too."

"Maybe we should go back, grab our phones, and come back here," Corinne said. "Emma might change her mind when we tell her what we found."

"Okay, let's do it," Andy said.

They made their way back to camp, but this time at a much faster pace.

***

Beth Hartley had never been what one would call a nature girl. Sure, sometimes her parents would take her to a local nature park, but nothing like where she was now. Shenandoah National Park was way more natural than she had ever encountered in her twenty-six years. Now, she was about to spend the weekend there with the man she pictured spending the rest of her life with. It was the first time she had been anywhere rural since she started her job eight months earlier.

Her heart beat with anticipation as she opened the door of her cabin. It was at the far end of a group of about ten cabins. Beth loved the shiny hardwood floors and the beautiful wood-paneled walls that matched the floors. It had an old-world charm that one never saw in the city. A fireplace stood in the center of the far wall. In front of that was the living room. To the left was a small kitchen, and to the right was the bedroom. Next to the bedroom was a bathroom. "This is awesome," Beth thought.

It was going to be a wonderful weekend. She brought along some wine with crackers and cheese. She thought they could sit by the fire while enjoying a glass of wine and a nice snack. She put the cheese in the refrigerator, brought her suitcase into the bedroom, unpacked it, and put everything in the dresser next to the bed. She brought a sexy negligee that she put on top of the dresser for easy access when the time was right.

She removed her business attire and hung them in the closet. She took off her bra and slipped on a T-shirt and shorts. She was about to call John when her phone rang. She picked it up, expecting it to be John telling her he was almost there, but it was her mother. "Hi, Mom."

"Hi, Honey. Did you make it to your cabin yet?"

"I just arrived a couple of minutes ago. It is beautiful here."

"That's nice. I'm glad you like it there. What about your boyfriend? Uh..."

"John. His name is John. I'm pretty sure I told you that several times."

"I'm sorry, Beth. I must be getting old."

"You're forty-nine, Mom. I think you still have a few good years left."

"I hope you're right. I want to live long enough to see my grandkids grow up."

"I am not ready to think about having kids yet, Mom."

"You will when you are with the right man."

"What are you talking about? I'm with the right man now."

"If that is true, why aren't you thinking about having kids?"

"I can't do this with you right now, Mom."

"I'm sorry, Honey. So, how does John like it there?"

"He's not here yet. He had some business to finish in Roanoke and should be here soon."

"Well, okay. I won't keep you. I just wanted to make sure you got to your cabin okay. Call me when you get home and let me know how everything went."

"I will, Mom. Thanks for calling. I love you."

"I love you too, Honey."

Beth hung up with her mother and picked up the phone to call John. She then had second thoughts and put the phone down. She didn't want to seem pushy. She looked at her watch and decided he must have finished what he needed to do by now, but why hadn't he called yet to let her know he was on the way?

She picked up her phone again and dialed John. He picked up on the third ring and said. "Hi, Beth. I'm sorry. I was about to call you. Something's come up, and I can't make it."

"What? What do you mean something's come up? Tell me you are not blowing me off. What has come up that's more important than spending a nice, quiet weekend with your girlfriend?"

"That's the thing, Beth."

Just then, Beth heard a woman's voice in the background. "Who are you talking to, John?"

"Who the hell is that?" Beth asked.

"I'm sorry, Beth. I wanted to tell you. I just didn't know how. I didn't want to hurt you."

"Well, you failed miserably, you asshole."

She hung up the phone. She wanted to throw it against the wall, but common sense prevailed, and she couldn't do it. She just sat on the bed and cried. She wanted to stop. She was far too tough a woman to be crying over a man. Maybe she wasn't as tough as she thought.

She lay there for a long time thinking about her life. She thought about all the mistakes she made and the mistakes she was not going to make in the future, men being one of them. Who needed them anyway? From now on, she was going to keep them at a distance. She would have sex when she wanted it, but no more commitments. It was better that way, both for her career and her happiness. She eventually fell into a deep sleep, waking up only once after having a nightmare about earthquakes, but quickly falling asleep again.

Chapter 2

The woman was gorgeous, Mike thought as she got out of the pool. Her wet, tan body glistened in the sun as she pushed her long, dark hair behind her head. Her ample breasts more than filled her tiny bikini. She approached Mike and said, "Are you going to just stand there, or are you going to hand me a towel?"

"Oh, yes. Of course. Here you go," Mike said as he handed her a towel.

She dried herself, dropped the towel, and stepped in very close. She put her hands on Mike's face and kissed him. "What would I do without you, Mike?" she said as she slowly unbuttoned his shirt.

"Mike. Mike. Wake up, Mike!"

Mike opened his eyes and saw his roommate, David Vargas, standing by his bed. "Dammit, Dave. I was just about to get laid."

"Sorry, Buddy, but you had all night for that. You need to get moving, or you're going to be late. How 'bout that earthquake last night? That was really something, huh?"

"Earthquake?"

"Yeah. A little before midnight. Are you telling me you slept through it?"

"I guess I did," Mike said.

"I thought you Army guys were light sleepers?"

"Maybe some are, but I served in Germany and North Carolina. Not exactly the front lines."

"You're still my hero," Dave said, laughing.

"Surely there must be something better you could be doing right now."

"Nope. Today's my day off."

"All right. All right," Mike said as he got out of bed and headed for the shower. When he finished showering, he brushed his teeth, shaved, and put his uniform on. He looked at himself in the mirror and was happy with his appearance. When he left the Army, he let himself go a little, but after eleven months with the National Park Service at Shenandoah, he was back in shape. The only thing he didn't like was his hair. His dark brown hair tended to get wavy when it grew past a certain length, and he was definitely past due for a haircut.

He put on his hat, packed his lunch box, and headed to his SUV parked outside. Almost immediately after starting his rounds, he encountered a group of visitors who flagged him down. They wanted to know what happened last night.

"Just a minor earthquake," Mike said. "Nothing to worry about."

***

Beth woke up later than usual. She was done crying. It was a new day and a chance to start fresh. She had the weekend off and was spending it in a beautiful park. She had never been anywhere like this before and knew she could enjoy herself even without the company of a man. She took a shower and got herself ready for the day.

She was getting hungry but only had crackers and cheese. She thought about going out for breakfast, but didn't know where to go. Instead, she made herself a cup of coffee and brought it outside to the front porch with the crackers and cheese. There were a couple of chairs there with a small table between them. She sat on one of the chairs and put her coffee on the table.

Since her cabin was at the end of a row of cabins, nature surrounded her on three sides. The air was thick with the fragrance of the forest. A feeling of tranquility swept over her as she listened to leaves rustling in the wind and the pleasant sounds of birds singing their songs to each other. She sat there drinking her coffee and snacking on the crackers and cheese. She couldn't remember the last time she felt this relaxed. She was used to the busy city life where everyone was always in a hurry. Waking up in the middle of a forest was quite a change for her, but she thought it was something she could get used to.

Her phone rang inside the cabin. She put the food on the table and went inside to answer it. She looked at the screen and saw it was her supervisor, Robert Klein. "Hello, sir," Beth said.

"Good morning, Beth. I hope I'm not disturbing you."

"No. It's fine. What's up?"

"Did you make it to Shenandoah? Are you there now?"

"I made it just fine. I'm here now. Thanks for asking."

"I'm sorry, but this isn't a social call. I know it's your day off, but I need to send someone down to Shenandoah. Since you are already there, I thought you might be willing to take the assignment. I don't want you to feel obligated. If you don't want it, I'll give it to someone else, but I was hoping you could at least get the ball rolling. If you do take it, feel free to take some time off after we resolve the issue."

"It's fine, sir. I'll take it. My plans here have changed anyway. What's going on?"

***

A little before noon, Mike was hungry, so he parked his vehicle and opened his lunch box. He had just started eating his sandwich when a call came over the radio. "Mike, you need to report to the visitor center right away."

"What's going on?" he asked.

"You'll find out when you get there."

He hated the vagueness. Why couldn't they just tell him? This wasn't the CIA, for God's sake. He took another bite of his sandwich and put it away. When he arrived at the visitor center, the park superintendent, Matthew Johnson, was there with a young woman. She was beautiful. She had long, straight, blond hair tied behind her head. She wore a black suit jacket, black pants, and a white shirt. She also wore black shoes with low heels. Not the best walking shoes, but much better than high heels.

"This is Ranger Michael Bauer," he said to the woman. "Mike, this is Agent Bethany Hartley. She's with the FBI. I would like you to work with her today."

They shook hands. "You can call me Beth," she said.

"You can call me Mike. What's this all about?"

Beth unlocked her phone and showed him a photo of a young woman. She had straight, medium-length dark brown hair and brown eyes. "Have you seen this woman?" she asked.

Mike looked at the photo and said, "No. I don't think so. Who is she?"

"Her name is Emma Drake. She is hiking the Appellation Trail with two friends. Her father reported her missing this morning."

"Seriously?" Mike said. "That's what this is about? Everyone on the trail is missing. That is why they are hiking the trail. They want to be missing. They are there for a peace you can't find in the city. Besides, a missing person is a matter for the police or sheriff, not the FBI."

"Normally, I would agree, but her father happens to be a United States Senator. I'm here to ensure she is okay and rule out any foul play."

"Foul play? Do you think someone would want to kidnap her?"

"I have no way of knowing that. I'm just here to find her. But since she is the daughter of a senator, the likelihood of a kidnapping goes up exponentially."

"What makes you so sure she's missing?"

"I'm not so sure. I was told to find her, and I intend to do that. What I know is that she has an arrangement with her father. She calls him every night when they make camp and texts him every morning when they leave camp."

"There are many areas of the trail that have no cell signal. Perhaps they are in one of those areas," Mike said.

"The senator is aware of that. She had a cell signal last night when she called her father, but didn't text him this morning. He tried calling her, but it went straight to voicemail. We tried tracing her phone, but it is either off or out of range."

"Maybe her battery is dead," Mike offered.

"I said everything you are saying right now to my superior, but her father insists she was monitoring the battery level closely. He said she only turns her phone on to contact him and then turns it off to save the battery. She also brought along a solar charger to charge it when needed. Besides, her hiking

11

companions also brought phones, but those are turned off or out of range, too."

The superintendent spoke up and said, "They were just past Blackrock Summit last night. Get down there and see what you can find."

"Of course, sir," Mike said. "Come with me," he said to Beth, leading her to his vehicle.

On the way, Mike asked. "Why did the FBI send only one agent for this? Don't you people usually work in pairs?"

"Usually, but not always. I suppose it is because I happened to be in the area. I also have a feeling they don't consider this as much of an emergency as her father does. They probably figured they would send the rookie so they could at least say they are doing something."

"Rookie, huh?" Mike said. "Me too. Well, I've been doing this for eleven months. I guess you're a rookie until you reach the year mark."

"Eight months for me," Beth said. "Three and a half if you don't count training."

"That's a lot of training. You have to count that. You'll get there soon, then the newbies will get the shit assignments."

"I don't consider this a shit assignment," Beth said. "Doing this alone gives me a chance to prove myself. When we find this girl alive and well, I'm sure the senator will be very grateful, which will, in turn, reflect well on me."

"That's a good way to look at it," Mike said. "Maybe that will work for me, too."

"Have you not proved yourself in eleven months?"

"I think I have, but having a grateful senator couldn't hurt. I mean, people pay a lot of money to have a senator in their pocket. All we have to do is find a girl."

Beth looked at Mike and said, "I take it you are not a fan of politicians."

"Not particularly. I'm sure many begin their careers with noble intentions before reality sets in. I don't see how anyone can get elected to a high office these days without owing favors to powerful people who do not have the best interests of the average citizen at heart.

"I guess you have a point, but there must be some good ones out there."

"I hope so."

When they arrived at their destination, Mike parked on the side of the road at a spot that he knew was closest to the trail. They got out and walked. After a couple of minutes, they were on the trail heading north. Beth said, "It's beautiful here. I can see what would attract someone to hiking."

"Have you ever hiked before?"

"No. Never. I've never even been camping. My mother hated camping, so we never went."

"How can anyone hate camping?"

"Not everyone is willing to give up the luxuries of modern life."

"I suppose that is true. Where did you grow up?" Mike asked.

"I'm a Florida girl. I grew up in Clearwater, not far from Tampa. I spent much of my free time at the beach, but anything resembling a forest was a world away."

"That's a shame," Mike said. "I grew up in West Virginia. The forest was my second home. The beach, on the other hand, was a world away."

"I guess a little of both would be nice," Beth said.

There was a bend in the trail, and when they came around the corner, they saw two men sitting on a log. They used their backpacks as makeshift tables while eating from tin plates. When they got close, Beth held out her phone and said, "Excuse me, gentlemen. We are looking for this young woman. Have you seen her?"

Both men stood up and looked at the photo. One of the men said, "Yes, I remember seeing her. She was with another man and a woman. They passed us a day or two ago, I think." He looked at his friend, who nodded in agreement and said, "It was yesterday morning. We were packing our stuff when they came by."

"You haven't seen them since then?" Mike asked.

"No. I'm afraid not," the first man said. The second man shook his head.

"What about other people? Did you see anyone pass you after they went by?" Beth asked.

"No. I'm pretty sure it was just them," the first man said. He looked at his partner, who nodded in agreement.

"Thank you so much," Beth said, and they continued walking. "I guess that means they are ahead of us somewhere."

"It's also possible they had no signal this morning, so they left without texting her dad. If that's the case, we'll have a long walk to catch up to them."

"For her sake, I hope you are right."

They walked and talked for another ten minutes, and then Mike saw it. In a clearing about twenty-five feet from the trail stood two small tents. They quickened their pace, and when they reached the tents, they noticed the remains of a campfire. They also found three backpacks. Two were inside one tent, and one was inside the other tent. Beth opened the single backpack. She rummaged around until she came up with a cell phone. She turned it on. Fortunately, the phone was not locked. She checked text messages and found what she was looking for. She held up the phone and said, "This is Emma's phone."

"That's strange," Mike said. "Why would they leave without their stuff?"

"Perhaps something scared them," Beth offered. "A bear, perhaps."

"If a bear chased them away, they would surely return or at least report it to someone. Even if the bear could kill one of them, it would certainly not get all three."

"We need to check the area," Beth said. "If someone kidnapped her, there might be clues nearby."

"So, do you think that's what happened?" Mike asked. "Do you think she really was kidnapped?"

"What else would explain the fact that their stuff is here, but they are not?"

"I don't know," Mike said. "You might be right. I can't think of any other reason they would leave without taking their belongings. It just seems like it would be difficult to kidnap someone while they are with friends. I suppose you could shoot the friends, but there are no bodies here."

"Maybe they kidnapped all three."

"I guess that's possible, but kidnapping one person would be much easier."

They walked for five minutes down the trail but saw nothing helpful. "We should go back to the tents and check the woods," Beth said.

When they returned, Mike pointed to his right and said, "Stay ten yards that way and never lose sight of me. Understand?"

"Yes," Beth said.

"Okay. Follow me, but watch where you are walking. There are rattlesnakes out here."

"Don't mess with me, Mike. I'm not in the mood."

"I'm not messing with you. There are rattlesnakes out here."

"I thought they were only out west."

"I think they have a different species out west. The ones here generally don't bother people, but if you were to surprise one or step on it, that's a different story."

As Beth walked into the woods, she watched her feet with every step. Mike watched her for a few seconds and said, "Wait! Wait! You won't find anything looking at your feet. Forget what I said. I wanted you to be aware of the snakes, but there is no need to fret over them."

"Who's fretting? I'm not fretting."

"It looked like fretting to me."

"I think you need glasses."

"Just keep your eyes open for anything unusual."

They walked about fifty yards into the woods until the ground started descending in a steep slope. "Wait there," Mike said. He walked toward Beth. When he reached her, he said, "Follow me," and they walked an additional ten yards.

"Wait here," he said before walking ten more yards away from Beth. "Now we are going to walk back towards the camp. Keep your eyes open for anything unusual."

They walked about twenty yards when Mike spotted it. It was ahead of him on his left. "I see something," he said. "Come this way."

"What do you see?" Beth asked as she made her way through the woods toward Mike.

"I can't tell from here," he said. "It might be a body."

They walked together until they came upon it. It was a body. It was a young man lying on his back. Dried blood covered his face and arms. He wore a light jacket that was ripped in several places, and his shirt was torn at the collar. Beth checked for a pulse. "He's cold," Beth said. "Probably died last night." She raised his hand for Mike to see. It looks like blood under his fingernails."

"Is this one of Emma's companions?" Mike asked.

Beth took out her phone, scrolled through her photographs, and found the one she was looking for. She looked at it closely and then looked at the body. "Yes, it's him. His name is Andrew Barber. It looks like he was in a fight, but with whom?"

Perhaps that will give us a clue, Mike said, pointing to another figure about fifteen yards away.

Beth looked at what he was pointing at and said, "Oh, shit. This is going from bad to worse."

They reached the second figure and saw it was another body. This one was face down, so Beth turned it over. It was a young woman. She also had ripped clothing and was covered in dried blood. Beth checked but knew she was also dead. She raised the young woman's hand to show she also had blood under her fingernails. She took out her phone and checked the photos. "It's not Emma," she said. "Her name is Corinne White. She was Emma's friend."

"This is getting worse by the minute," Mike said. "Do you think maybe Emma was kidnapped, and her friends got in the way? Maybe they tried to defend her."

"That is one possibility," Beth said. "At this point, I would prefer that to finding her body out here, too."

"It seems weird that they are so far from their tents. I would think the kidnappers would approach them at their camp, and any resistance would take place nearby."

"Maybe they ran, and the kidnappers chased them down."

"We need to keep looking," Mike said. "Same as before. You go ten yards that way and keep pace with me."

They got into position and headed back into the woods. When they reached the steep downward slope, Beth said, "I see something."

Mike went to her and saw a body about fifty feet down the hill. "Stay here," he said. "It's dangerous. I'll go check it out."

Beth ignored Mike and followed him down the hill. They found a young woman with several bruises on her body and a gash on her forehead. "It's her. It's Emma," Beth said.

Mike reached her first and checked for a pulse. "She's alive," he said and opened his phone to get the GPS location. He took out his radio, called in his location, and said he had a severely injured young woman who needed an emergency evacuation. He also reported the two dead bodies they found.

Beth gently touched the young woman's shoulder and said, "Emma! Emma!"

"She must have fallen down the hill and hit her head on that tree there," Mike said.

"I need her to tell us what happened," Beth said.

"I'm afraid you can't force that. You will have to wait until she wakes up."

"If she wakes up," Beth said.

Chapter 3

After Emma was extracted from the ravine and airlifted to the hospital, Mike said to Beth, "So, I guess you'll be heading back to Washington or wherever you came from."

"Hell no. I'm not leaving now," Beth said. "The people who did this to them are still out there. I need to find them, or they might try again."

"Do you still think someone tried to kidnap Emma?"

"That is the only logical scenario I can come up with unless you have another idea."

"I'm afraid I don't, but if someone tried to kidnap her, why didn't they go down the hill and get her?"

"Who knows? Maybe it was dark. Maybe she ran from them, and they lost her after she fell down the hill."

"I guess that's possible," Mike said. "Okay, if you are going to stay, we need to set you up with accommodations."

Beth held up a key and said, "No need. I already have a cabin."

Mike looked at the key and said, "If you know the cabin number, I can show you where it is."

"No. Thank you. I've already been there."

"Really? You went to your cabin first?"

"Are you judging me?" Beth asked.

"No. I just figured you would want to find the girl first. Plus, you might have wrapped this up in one day and not needed a place to stay."

"I don't think I need to explain myself to you."

"No, you certainly do not, and I'm sorry I brought it up."

They walked back to Mike's SUV and drove to the visitor center. Before they got out, Beth said, "Do you want to see where my cabin is in case we will be working together tomorrow? You might want to know where you can pick me up."

Mike could have found it easily by knowing her cabin number, but said, "Good idea. I'll follow you."

Beth got in her car, and Mike followed her to her cabin. When they arrived, Beth unlocked the door, and they both walked inside. "This is a beautiful cabin. I bet you wish you had gone camping before now," Mike said.

"This is not exactly what I would call camping," Beth said.

"Hey, you have to crawl before you can walk. You are still able to enjoy the great outdoors here. You just have a roof over your head and a bathroom."

"And a comfortable bed, a television, a stove, and a refrigerator."

"Okay, Okay. I see your point. It's still better than the city."

"It sure is. Well, thank you for everything, Mike. Do you think we will be working together again tomorrow?"

"I will make sure of it. For now, though, you must be hungry, and I doubt anyone stocked your refrigerator. If you want, I'll take you to town and show you where you can pick up supplies. I'll even buy you dinner."

Beth smiled and said, "My pride wants to refuse your offer, but my stomach says, 'Show me the food.'"

"Does your stomach always win?"

"Pretty much, unfortunately."

Mike didn't know if she was referring to a problem with her weight. If she was, he couldn't see it. He decided not to say anything about it. "Okay, then. Let's go."

They drove for about twenty minutes and parked in front of a pizza restaurant near the middle of town. "I hope you like pizza," Mike said.

"I feel like you know me already."

They went inside and were seated near the back. The place was packed with people. They decided on a medium supreme pizza, and they both ordered a beer.

"I'm surprised you ordered a beer," Mike said.

"Why? It's Saturday night. Do you think FBI agents are not allowed to drink?"

"No. It just seems that most women don't like beer. They tend to order wine or one of those fufu drinks."

"Fufu drinks?"

"You know what I mean."

"Yes, I think I do, and I think you've been hanging out with the wrong women."

Mike smiled and said, "It seems you know me already, too."

"That doesn't sound good," Beth said. "Have you been having girl troubles?"

"Well, let's see. My high school sweetheart cheated on me with my former best friend. My fiancé suddenly decided that she liked girls better than boys, and my most recent serious relationship turned into a nightmare. I didn't realize it at first, but she was psychotic."

"Psychotic? What did she do that was psychotic?"

"She was extremely jealous and would scrutinize everything I did. She would look through my phone and my computer. She would accuse me of sleeping around without any evidence. She acted as if she knew I had done something wrong, but remained vague about what she supposedly knew. I'm sure she hoped I would confess to something, even though I never knew what she was talking about. I finally couldn't take it anymore and broke up with her. Even after I broke up with her, she stalked me for weeks. I considered getting a restraining order, but she soon found a new boyfriend to harass and forgot about me."

"Some jealous women can be dangerous. At least you made it out in one piece," Beth said.

"I was lucky. All my army training couldn't prepare me for a jealous woman. What about you? Is there a man in your life?"

"Not at the moment," Beth said. "I think I had slightly better luck than you, but with the same result. My first love interest, if you can call it that, was a boy I knew in my sophomore year of high school. His family picked up and moved out of state after the school year ended, and I never saw him again. I dated a guy in college, but it was more of a friends-with-benefits situation. After graduation, we went our separate ways. Since joining the FBI, I have been too busy for a serious relationship. I did try once recently, but it didn't work out."

"It didn't work because you were too busy?" Mike asked.

"No. It seems I was the flavor of the month. When the month changed, so did the flavor."

"I'm sorry. That guy was an asshole. Pretty stupid, too. I mean, you seem like quite a catch. Why would he let you go?"

"Thank you, Mike. I think he didn't want to have any commitments. After we broke up, I thought long and hard about where my life was going and concluded that he had done the right thing. The best thing I can do now is follow his lead and live for myself. If I want to get ahead, I must focus all my energy on my career."

"That's messed up on so many levels," Mike said.

"After what you told me, I would hardly consider you a relationship expert. What is wrong with putting me first?"

"First, I never said I was a relationship expert, but I know a little about being happy. Second, you will never be happy with the attitude that you have adopted. Sure, you might get what you want quicker, but once you get it, you will be disappointed because of how unsatisfying it feels. Third, the goal in life is to be happy, not to accumulate things, make a lot of money, or climb the corporate ladder. If you want to be happy, the number one way is to do whatever you can to improve the lives of others."

"Oh, really? So if I gave all my money and possessions to charity, that would make me happy?"

"No. Of course not. You can't hurt yourself in the process. You just have to be kind to people. You need to love people, sometimes intimately and sometimes as friends. Loving someone not only helps you to be happy, but it also improves the happiness level of the person you love. If you give up on love, you also give up on happiness."

"I can tell you are passionate about this subject, Mike, but I'm not convinced."

"Well, if you do nothing else, at least make time to have fun occasionally. It's not good for you to be all work and no play."

The waitress arrived and set their beers in front of them. "Your pizza will be up shortly," she said. "Is there anything I can get you?"

"No. Thank you," Mike said.

When she walked away, Beth said, "I like to play."

"You like to play, but do you?"

"Of course I do," Beth insisted.

"Okay, what have you done that would be considered fun in the last three months?"

"I've done plenty," Beth said.

"Tell me. Name one thing."

"Well, there was, um. You know, I didn't come here to be interrogated."

Mike laughed and said, "Okay. I'm sorry. Let's change the subject."

"Good idea," Beth said.

"So, what do you like to do with the little free time that you have?" Mike asked.

"I don't know. I guess I enjoy reading."

"That's good. What kind of books do you like?"

"You know, the usual: Psychological Profiling, Murder for Dummies. Books like that."

"I'm going to assume you are joking," Mike said just before the pizza arrived.

Mike pulled off a couple of pieces and put them on Beth's plate, then took a couple of pieces for himself. Beth took a bite and said, "This is very good."

"I thought you would like it. This is my favorite restaurant in town."

Beth took another bite of pizza and said, "I can see why."

***

Tom and Jill Meyers pulled their motorhome into Shenandoah National Park an hour before sunset. Tom retired two years earlier, and Jill retired last summer. When she did, they sold their house and bought the motorhome. It wasn't huge by any means, but it was big enough for them. They spent the winter in Florida, changing their location every month or so. They didn't like to make reservations. They wanted the freedom to move on whenever the place they were staying at became stale. Of course, that meant many places were full, but they always managed to find somewhere to stay.

They worked their way south along the west coast of Florida and then north along the east coast. When winter turned to spring, they left Florida. They last stayed in Myrtle Beach, South Carolina, before ending up at Shenandoah. Jill's hairdresser in Myrtle Beach suggested it. She heard from her daughter-in-law that her sister said it was a great place to camp. They figured they would try it. If they didn't like it there, they could always leave.

Tom pulled out their portable fire pit from the storage area when they finished setting everything up. He placed it at the suggested minimum distance, and they put their lawn chairs near it. The only thing left to do was get firewood.

The sun had gone down, but Tom figured it would be light long enough to get what he needed. He walked to the edge of the tree line but saw nothing useful there, so he headed into the trees. He found several large twigs and small branches that would probably burn well, but he needed more. He continued deeper into the woods and spotted a branch that was just what he needed. He bent down to pick it up. When he did, he heard a twig snap. He stood up and turned around just in time to see a large black paw slash him across the face.

***

Mike drove to a nearby grocery store after they left the pizza restaurant. There, Beth picked up a case of water and several snacks. When they returned to Mike's SUV, Beth asked, "Is the hospital where they took Emma nearby?"

"It's not too far," Mike said. "Maybe fifteen minutes."

"Do you mind taking me there? I want to check on her."

"No problem," Mike said and drove to the hospital. When they arrived, someone told them to go to the third floor. Once there, a nurse directed them to room 315. A police officer stood outside the door. Beth showed her identification to the officer, and they went inside. Emma was awake and sitting up in bed, talking to her parents.

Beth held up her identification and said, "Hi. I'm Agent Beth Hartley, and this is Ranger Mike Bauer. You must be Senator and Mrs. Drake."

"That's right," the senator said. Are you the ones who found Emma?"

"Yes. Yes, we did," Beth said.

"We are so very grateful to both of you," Mrs. Drake said.

"We are just happy she is okay," Beth said.

"Did you learn anything about who did this?" Senator Drake asked.

"No," Beth said. "We came here hoping to talk to Emma about that."

Emma said, "I'm sorry, but I don't remember anything. Is it true what they say? Are Corinne and Andy dead?"

Beth nodded slowly and said, "I'm afraid so. I'm so sorry."

She started crying and then forced herself to calm down. When she was able to speak, she said, "What happened? Who killed them?"

"We are working on figuring that out," Beth said. "Are you sure you don't remember anything?"

"The last thing I remember was setting up camp. Everything after that is a blur."

"What do you mean by a blur? Do you remember something?" Beth asked.

"Well, it's going to sound crazy, but I vaguely remember a fireball."

"A fireball?" Beth said and looked at Mike, who shrugged.

"I told you it was crazy. I can't explain it. It's just stuck in my mind, like a dream."

"We are so glad you are okay," Beth said. "If you remember anything, please let us know."

"I will," Emma said. "I am grateful to both of you for finding me out there."

Beth smiled and said. "You can thank your dad for notifying us."

Beth took out her business card and handed it to the senator. "If she remembers anything, no matter how trivial, please call me."

"I will," he said, "and thank you again for saving our daughter. I owe you one."

When they left, Beth said, "What do you think she meant by 'fireball?'"

"I don't know. Maybe she had a dream and confused it with reality," Mike said.

"I suppose that could be it."

Mike drove Beth back to her cabin. As they said their goodbyes, Mike wanted to kiss her goodnight, as if they had just returned from a date. He resisted that urge, knowing it was not a date. She was an agent investigating a possible kidnapping attempt, and he was a ranger assigned to assist her. Ultimately, they both just said goodbye, and Mike returned to his cabin.

Chapter 4

Mike showed up at Beth's cabin early the following morning. He was surprised to see her dressed and ready to go. He was even more surprised that she discarded her FBI clothes for blue jeans and a casual blouse. "There's been a bear attack," he said. "I've been ordered to help in the search for the bear, so I won't be able to help you today, or at least not until we find the bear."

"Is the person okay?" Beth asked.

"I'm afraid he didn't make it."

"Oh, jeez. That's terrible. Is there anything I can do to help?"

"Not really, but I don't see why you couldn't tag along. That is if you want to."

"Give me two minutes," she said. She went inside, put on her holster, and slid her gun into it. She then put her suit jacket over it and met Mike outside.

He looked at her and said, "Are you going for the casual business attire look?"

"It's a long story."

Mike looked down at her shoes and said, "You have tennis shoes. Are those FBI issue?

"I told you it's a long story. Let's just go."

"Okay, then," Mike said before getting in his vehicle. Beth slid into the passenger seat, and Mike drove to the camping area where the attack took place.

On the way, Mike thought about how Beth was dressed and finally said. "I think I understand."

"You understand what?"

"You told me after we met that you were chosen for this assignment because you were already nearby. You weren't nearby. You were here, weren't you? That explains why you had already been to your cabin and why you only have one work outfit. Why would you worry about that information getting out? So you came here on vacation and got roped into working. What's the big deal?"

"The big deal is, Sherlock, I don't need to tell you everything about my life."

Mike smiled and said, "Your ex-boyfriend. How long has he been an ex?"

"Why are you so interested in my personal life? You should leave it alone."

"You were supposed to meet your boyfriend here, but he stood you up for that new flavor of the month, didn't he?"

"Yes! Okay? Are you happy? You figured it out. You get a gold star," Beth said before turning to look out the window.

"I'm sorry," Mike said. "I'm sorry about your shitty boyfriend, and I'm sorry for being so nosy. I shouldn't have pushed it."

Beth looked back at him and said, "You are right. You shouldn't have pushed it, but I have to admit I'm impressed with your reasoning skills. Don't let this go to your head, but perhaps your boss knew what he was doing when he picked you to work with me."

Mike smiled but didn't reply.

There was a makeshift command center set up near the dead man's motor home. When they arrived, Mike took a rifle out of the trunk and slung it over his shoulder. He then took out a tranquilizer pistol and tucked it into his waistband. The

31

superintendent was there and looked surprised to see Beth. "Good morning, Agent Hartley," he said. "I'm afraid this has nothing to do with your investigation."

"Are you sure?" Beth asked.

"Yes. This was a bear attack, completely unrelated to the senator's daughter."

"Well, I still want to help. Another set of eyes couldn't hurt."

"It could be dangerous. I can't guarantee your safety."

Beth patted her side where her gun was and said, "I'll be fine."

"Suit yourself," he said. He then pulled out a map and showed Mike where he wanted him to search.

Mike motioned for Beth to follow. He said, "It's not far. We can walk. The trail runs through the middle of our search area, so it should be relatively easy."

After about ten minutes of walking, they reached the trail and headed south. Beth asked, "Is it common for bears to attack humans around here?"

"Something like this has never happened since I have been here," Mike said. "Occasionally, you hear about a bear invading someone's campsite and stealing their food, but that's usually the worst. They are not aggressive towards humans like grizzly bears are."

"Until now," Beth said.

"Yes. Until now."

"So, what would make a black bear attack a human?"

"A mother protecting her cubs would be the first thing that comes to mind. A bear might also attack if someone surprises or harasses it. The most concerning reason, although it is rare, is a bear that has a mental disorder or rabies, which usually don't occur in bears, but it is possible."

"Having a crazy bear loose around people is a scary thought, but what if it is as simple as a bear defending her young?" Beth asked. "Will the bear be destroyed if we find it, and what will become of the young bears?"

"If we find it, I plan to tranquilize it. What happens later will be out of our hands, but I'm sure they will factor everything in."

"Besides days like today, do you like working as a forest ranger?" Beth asked.

"Technically, I'm a park ranger and love what I do. I get to spend my days outdoors in nature. I also get to meet many interesting people. Of course, I do occasionally have to deal with someone who has had too much to drink or someone who is doing something stupid and dangerous. Often, they are the same person. What about you? Do you like your job?"

"Sure. Of course." Beth said.

"That didn't sound very convincing."

"I do like my job. Sometimes I feel like I'm making a real difference."

"Only sometimes? What about the other times?"

"I don't know. I suppose it just feels like things are too political at times. In this case, for example, if the daughter of a truck driver or a school teacher went missing, I would not be here."

"There will always be important people and unimportant people. I wish that weren't the case, but you can't change human nature."

"I suppose you're right. I'm probably drawing conclusions more from feelings than real evidence."

"Feelings are important too. What we call feelings or intuition is our brain running subroutines in the background and coming up with an answer before we can even ask the question."

"You seem to know a lot for a park ranger."

"Do you think park rangers are not intelligent?"

"No. I don't think that at all. I mean that you seem knowledgeable outside of your chosen career."

"Well, I like to read too."

They turned a corner and saw two men standing about five feet off the trail. One man looked to be in his early forties. He wore a backpack and was looking at a tablet computer. The other man was in his early twenties. He also wore a backpack and carried a metal detector. The backpacks were nothing like the ones that hikers carried. They were more like the backpacks that students carried their books to school in. When they got closer, the older man said, "Good morning, Ranger. Good morning, ma'am."

"Good morning," Mike said. "Do you mind if I ask what you two are doing?"

"Oh, we're from the university. "I'm Doctor Brown. Most of my students call me Doctor Mark. My name's Mark Brown. My students used to call me Doc Brown, but I try to discourage that now. Too many people ask where I keep my DeLorean. Well, anyway, I guess I'm rambling. This is a student of mine, James Black. He was very close to having my last name, which would have been equally troublesome for him. Um, well, I

34

guess you don't care about any of that. We are here looking for the meteorite that struck this area the night before last."

"Meteorite?" Mike said. He thought momentarily and said, "That wasn't a meteorite. That was a small earthquake."

"I don't know where you got your information, but it was definitely a meteorite strike. That's what caused the tremor everyone felt."

Mike was not going to mention that he slept through it, so he said, "Do you know where this meteorite hit?"

"Not exactly," the man said. "We are pretty sure it fell within a half-mile from our location, but we have no idea yet in which direction."

"Is this something people need to be concerned with?" Mike asked. "I mean, can they be radioactive or something?"

"They are generally harmless. Sometimes they can contain trace amounts of radioactive material, but almost always in quantities far too low to harm anyone."

"Even so, I need to know if you find it." Mike handed the man his business card. "That has the main number on it. Call it if you find something. We need to keep people away from it until we know for certain it's safe."

He looked at the card and said, "Okay, Ranger Mike. We will certainly keep you posted on what we find."

"What's the metal detector for?" Beth asked.

"Meteorites often have a high metallic content," Doctor Brown said. "If the dirt is soft enough, it can bury itself underground. The metal detector will help us know where to dig."

"You might want to put your search on hold until tomorrow. We had a bear attack in the park, and we haven't found the bear yet," Mike said. "It could be dangerous out in the woods."

"We'll be careful," the man said, tapping his backpack. "We brought bear spray."

"I hope that's enough," Mike said before he and Beth continued walking.

"There must be a full moon," Beth said. "There is a lot of craziness going on around here. Two murders, a kidnapping attempt, a bear attack, and a meteorite strike."

"It's been a hell of a couple of days. At least we know now what Emma meant by a fireball. They must have been up late and saw it."

"Do you think that meteorite has something to do with everything that has happened?" Beth asked.

"Anything is possible, but I don't see how. I'm sure all of this is just a big coincidence. By the way, did you learn anything about the death of Emma's friends?"

Beth took out her phone and said, "I expect to learn something soon." She checked her messages but saw nothing new. She then noticed her phone had no service. "There's no service here. I guess I won't know anything until we get a signal again."

"Hopefully, we, or somebody, will find that bear soon," Mike said.

"Hopefully," Beth agreed. "Then I can get back to my mission."

"Tell me, Beth, what made you want to join the FBI?"

"I don't know. Maybe it was Dana Scully."

"Dana Scully?"

"Yeah. You know, from the X-Files."

"Oh, yes. The redhead."

"Exactly, but I don't think she is a redhead in real life. Anyway, I used to watch reruns of the show when I was a young teenager. I felt like she was a lot like me, or I was like her. I mean, she was the analytical one. Mulder was always suggesting some supernatural explanation for things, but she would stop him and try to come up with a sensible, scientific answer. Of course, I'm not a scientist, but I believe my strength is my ability to look at things from multiple angles."

"You're in the right job for that."

"What about you?" Beth asked. "Why did you become a park ranger?"

"Well, after college, I joined the Army. I was in the military police. When I got out, I went to work for my brother in his furniture business, but it wasn't for me. At the same time, I was dealing with my ex stalking me. I started thinking of leaving and going somewhere peaceful. I thought it would be nice to get a small camper and live in the woods, but naturally, I would need money, so I eventually decided that a job as a park ranger would be a great fit for me. By then, the crazy ex had moved on, but I had made up my mind. Fortunately, my degree in law enforcement and the fact that I was a veteran helped me get the job."

"Why didn't you try to get a job in law enforcement after you got out?"

"At the time, it had just lost its appeal to me."

Just then, Mike noticed something. "Look, footprints," he said, pointing at the ground in front of them.

Beth didn't see them at first, but after a few seconds of looking, she noticed a couple of slight indentations in the dirt.

"You have good eyes. I would have missed that. Are those from a bear?"

"They look about the right size, but the hard dirt doesn't leave much detail."

"I can't tell. Which way was it going?"

Mike pointed to the left. "That way."

The trees were somewhat thin in that area, but there was no sign of a bear. Mike took his rifle off his shoulder and said, "Follow me and stick close. Be ready for anything. We don't want this bear to surprise us. That's assuming it is a bear."

Beth took out her handgun and followed Mike into the woods. After a hundred feet or so, Mike spotted another footprint to their right and said, "Look. That is almost certainly a bear print."

They followed the prints. It wasn't easy. It wasn't like following tracks in the snow. The ground had to be just right for a bear to leave a footprint, so the footprints were few and far between. Mike scanned the ground as far as he could see left and right for any sign that something big had passed by. Ten minutes later, Beth saw it first. "What's that over there?" she asked, pointing ahead and to the right.

Mike looked and saw something black and unmoving in the distance. He put a finger in front of his lips, and they moved forward as quietly as possible. When they were within a hundred feet, Mike whispered, "It's a bear. It looks like it's sleeping." He handed Beth his rifle and said, "I assume you know how to use this."

"Of course," she said as she put her pistol away and took the rifle.

Mike took out his tranquilizer gun, and they moved forward again. Mike was about to fire at twenty feet but stopped and said, "I don't think it's breathing."

They both moved in closer. Beth kept the rifle trained on the bear, just in case. When Mike was close enough, he pushed the bear with his foot and quickly backed away. Nothing happened. He moved in close again and placed his hand on the bear's abdomen, but he could feel no breathing. He then felt its paw. It was cold. "This bear is dead," he said, and Beth relaxed.

Mike put his tranquilizer gun back in his pants, and Beth handed his rifle back to him, which he slung over his shoulder. "What the hell is going on around here?" she asked.

"I have no idea," he said as he examined the bear's body. "There is no sign of trauma. This bear just died."

"I have a bad feeling about this," Beth said. "We need to get somewhere that has a cell signal. I need to find out what killed Emma's friends. I'm starting to doubt it was a kidnapping attempt."

"I agree. That is starting to look unlikely."

Mike used his radio and called in the location of the dead bear. They then returned to where they started without waiting for anyone to show up. When they arrived, Superintendent Johnson was still there. He said, "Good job finding that bear, you two."

"Thank you, sir," Mike said. "I think something weird is going on around here. Whatever it is could be a danger to everyone. You may want to consider closing this area down until we learn more."

"I've considered that already, Mike, but I need more than a few isolated incidents."

"I'll take Agent Hartley back to her cabin so she can make some calls. If we can find out what killed those two hikers, maybe we will have a better understanding of what is going on. I would also put a rush on finding the cause of death of that bear."

"I understand you were a good investigator in the Army," Johnson said. "I'm putting this in your hands. Figure out what's going on here. The sooner, the better."

"I'll do my best, sir," Mike said. He then added, "With Agent Hartley's help, of course."

***

Doctor Brown formulated a search pattern in his head and directed James on where to go. They spent several hours walking back and forth through the forest, using the trail as a center point. Some of the walking was easy, but other areas were very dense, and they had to alter their direction several times. Finally, James noticed the tops of some trees were broken, so they headed in that direction. They followed the broken trees until they reached a clearing. In the clearing sat exactly what they were looking for.

They walked to the edge of the crater caused by the meteorite and stood for a moment. "There it is. Isn't she beautiful?" Doctor Brown said.

"She sure is," said James.

The crater was bigger than Doctor Brown expected. The meteorite was also bigger than he expected. Only the top third of it was visible. The rest was buried under the dirt, but enough could be seen for Doctor Brown to estimate its size. He thought it was about the same size as the V8 in his old Lincoln Town Car. He bought it twenty years earlier, shortly after he accepted the job with the university. He loved that car, but traded it in after a few years because people started worrying about global warming and acted like he was the leading cause of it. He started driving a Prius, which he found uncomfortable, but at least he didn't have to listen to any crap from his students.

"C'mon, James," he said, stepping down into the soft dirt.

When they got close, Doctor Brown put his hand about an inch from the meteorite. He wanted to make sure it wasn't too hot to touch. After not feeling any heat emanating from it, he touched it with his fingertips. It felt warm but not hot. He removed his backpack, took out a small hammer and chisel, and said. "It's too big to take with us. We need to get samples and then get help to remove it."

He removed a small glass jar from his backpack, unscrewed the lid, and set it down. He chipped off three small pieces from different parts of the rock, put the pieces in the jar, closed the lid, and put the jar back in his backpack. "Let's head back," he said.

They walked back toward the trail. A little after reaching the halfway point, James asked, "Are we going to let that ranger know we found the meteorite?"

"Hell, no!" Doctor Brown said. "They just want the glory of the find. I'm not going to let them have it. I can't wait to see the look on Dr. Jerkowitz's face when he sees what I found."

"I think you mean Dr. Berkowitz," James said, "and we both found it."

"Don't be a credit hog, James."

"Credit hog? What do you think you're doing right now?"

"I'm in charge here. Do you think Columbus shared credit for his discovery with his shipmates? Why should he? He was the leader."

"That's probably because Columbus was a dick, just like you."

Doctor Brown took off his backpack and put it on the ground. He pushed his index finger into James's chest and said, "You take that back."

James dropped the metal detector, removed his backpack, and pushed Dr. Brown with both hands. "Don't touch me," he said.

"I'll touch you whenever I want," Dr. Brown said, pushing James even harder.

James returned with a punch to the stomach, making Doctor Brown curl over in pain, gasping for air. When he recovered enough, he grabbed a handful of dirt and threw it in James's face. He then jumped on him, forcing them both to the ground. They rolled back and forth on the ground, each punching the other in the head, trying to reach a dominant position. Suddenly, Doctor Brown went limp. He said, "I fight you want no more. You water are. Half fill in glass."

James suddenly came to his senses. He stood up and saw Doctor Brown just lying there with a confused look on his face.

James felt the beginning of a headache that steadily got worse. He put his hands on his head, but it didn't help much. He took out his phone to call 911, but it had no signal. "Dammit!" he screamed and threw his phone hard against a tree. It soon became difficult to breathe, and James felt as if his heart was going to explode out of his chest. He sat beside Doctor Brown, hoping the feeling would disappear.

Chapter 5

Mike and Beth drove back to Beth's cabin and went inside. Beth took out her phone and saw she had a couple of bars, so she opened her contact list and dialed a number. Mike only heard her side of the conversation. "Yes, I was out of cell phone range. I just got back. What? Are you sure? What about the injuries? Okay, thanks."

She hung up the phone, and Mike asked, "What did they say?"

"They both died from an aneurysm."

"An aneurysm? That can't be. It looked like someone beat the hell out of them."

"I agree, but that's what the coroner said. He said Corinne White died from an abdominal something or other aneurysm, and Andy Barber died from a cerebral aneurysm."

"Did he say what caused it?"

"He doesn't know yet. He's waiting for the toxicology report. He should have that soon."

"What about their injuries?"

"He will let us know when he gets his reports."

"Where did they take the bodies?"

"They're in Roanoke," Beth said.

"We should go there and talk to the medical examiner in person. By the time we get there, he should know more."

"We can't do much from here right now anyway, so let's go. I'll drive."

"You don't like my driving?" Mike asked.

"Are you kidding? You either drive like an old lady or Mario Andretti."

"I don't drive that badly. You just like being in control, which you can't do from the passenger seat."

"Are you a forest ranger or Sigmund Freud?"

"I'm a park ranger, not a forest ranger."

"Whatever."

They walked out to Beth's car. It was a blue Ford Edge. After they got inside, Mike said, "I thought you FBI people all drove black sedans."

Beth started the car, looked at Mike, and said, "I hope you don't get all your information from television shows."

"Of course not," Mike said. "Just the important stuff."

Beth smiled and then shook her head. "Well, if you fail as a forest, I mean park ranger, you can always get a job as a comedian."

"I'll save you a seat in the front row."

"You can tell people you were in the Army and you were a ranger. That should impress them right off the bat."

"They should be impressed," Mike said. "I was trained to be able to arrest an Army Ranger."

"That seems hard to believe," Beth said. "Are you telling me you have arrested Army Rangers?"

"No. I said I was trained to be able to arrest an Army Ranger. So far, I've never met one who deserved to be arrested."

"I hope you never will."

"Are you worried that I can't handle myself?"

"I didn't say that."

Mike decided to change the subject and said, "You know, we haven't eaten all day, and I'm getting hungry."

"I'm hungry too. I'll stop somewhere soon."

Ten minutes later, Beth got off the highway and pulled into a McDonald's drive-thru.

"McDonald's?" Mike said. "I was thinking a little better than that."

"I just thought we could get a little something to hold us over, or did you want me to look for a fancy restaurant where you can get steak and lobster?"

"That would be great," Mike said. "I'm sure the FBI gives you a nice little expense account."

"So, do you want a Big Mac or a fish sandwich?"

Mike sighed and said, "You're a cheap date. I guess I'll have a Big Mac."

"Good choice," Beth said.

They got their food and were back on the highway five minutes later. Mike took a bite of his burger and said, "Thank you for lunch."

"It's your turn to buy next time. Do you know any good restaurants that serve steak and lobster?"

"Oh, you can join me on that comedy tour."

They arrived at the coroner's office a little less than an hour later. They went inside and asked to speak with the medical examiner. After a few minutes, he greeted them and invited them into his office. He was about forty years old, of average height, with hair cut very short. It had receded quite a bit, but he did not try to hide that fact. "You're here about the two victims from the park, right?"

"Yes," Beth said. "Corinne White and Andy Barber."

He found their files and opened them. "I just got the toxicology reports, but haven't had a chance to look at them. Give me a couple of minutes, please."

"Of course," Beth said.

He looked at the report for Andy and then checked the report for Corinne. He looked back and forth several times and then wrote some things on a piece of paper and thought for a moment.

Beth and Mike looked at each other but said nothing.

Finally, he said, "I told you on the phone that both the victims suffered an aneurysm. The cause of that was extremely high and prolonged levels of adrenaline. What caused those high levels of adrenaline is still unknown. The victims had trace amounts of several toxins in their bodies. Keep in mind that almost all humans have trace amounts of several toxins, but some of these are elevated higher than normal. The ones they have in common that are slightly higher than normal are lead, mercury, beryllium, and one that is not in our database."

"None of these by themselves could cause what we have seen with these victims, except maybe the unknown compound. It is also possible that certain chemicals in combination might be the culprit. Unfortunately, there has not been widespread testing of the effects of different chemicals when combined."

"Or, fortunately, if you are the test subject," Mike said.

"Touché," said the medical examiner.

"What about the cuts and bruising?" Beth asked.

"Oh yes," he said. "They each had the other's blood and skin under their fingernails."

Mike looked at Beth and back at the medical examiner. "You mean they fought each other?"

"It would seem so. I would guess that their elevated adrenaline levels, or whatever caused it, amped them up so high that the slightest disagreement turned into a slugfest. That probably caused their already racing hearts to pump harder than their arteries could handle."

"There was a third person who didn't have the same symptoms," Beth said.

"I can't explain that," the medical examiner said. "That person must not have been exposed to whatever caused this. Perhaps they were separated at some point."

"The meteorite," Mike said. "When they saw the meteorite crash, perhaps Corinne and Andy went to check it out, but Emma stayed behind. Maybe she was scared to go into the forest at night."

"That makes sense," Beth said. "I think you might make a good investigator someday."

"Thanks a lot," Mike said.

"Doctor, do you think a meteorite could cause the high levels of toxins in their systems?" Beth asked.

"I'm no expert, but I would guess maybe some of the heavy metals."

"What about the unknown chemical?"

"I couldn't answer that. You would have to ask an astronomer or geologist or whoever studies meteorites," he said.

"Thank you so much for your time, Doctor. You've been a big help," Beth said.

When they returned to the car, Mike asked, "If Andy and Corinne got into a fight, how was Emma involved? How did she end up falling down that hill?"

"We may never know that. Perhaps she tried to break up their fight, and they turned on her. Maybe they chased her into the woods, but collapsed before they could reach her."

"I suppose that is probably what happened or something similar,"

Mike called Superintendent Johnson. "Hi Mike, what did you find?" he asked.

"We just left the medical examiner's office. We learned that the two victims we found died from aneurysms caused by excessive adrenaline. Some unknown combination of heavy metals and or toxins caused that. The medical examiner said they had low levels of several heavy metals along with a compound that they couldn't identify. We believe they witnessed the meteorite strike the other night and went to check it out. It's possible that something in that meteorite is affecting animals and people who get too close. Maybe the dead bear got too close to that meteorite."

"If that's true, we could have a major problem here," Johnson said.

"I think you should close down that section of the park, sir."

"I appreciate your concern, son, but that is a big step. It's early June, and we will have a horde of hikers coming through here soon. Should I tell them, 'Sorry, I know you've been hiking for six weeks, but you have to turn back now?'"

"What's more important, their hike or their lives?" Mike asked.

"You're right," said Johnson. "The welfare of the visitors and staff is my top priority. The problem is I have people to answer to. I need more evidence. For now, we will increase patrols and inform people to be extra vigilant. Once I learn the bear's cause of death, I will make a final determination then."

"When will you know?" Mike asked.

"We should know something by tomorrow morning, I would imagine."

"Okay. Please let me know as soon as you know something," Mike said.

***

"When they got back on the road, Mike said, "So, I guess this means you'll be leaving."

"Leaving? Why would I leave?"

"Because it's pretty obvious that nobody was ever here to kidnap Emma Drake."

"It's obvious to you, but somebody could have injected them with something."

Mike looked at Beth and said. "You don't believe that. You just want to spend more time with me."

"Don't flatter yourself," Beth said. "I just want to see this through."

Mike just leaned back and smiled.

Beth looked at him and said, "You can wipe that smug look off your face. I am not staying because of you."

"If you say so," Mike said and smiled again.

Beth just shook her head but said nothing.

"Hey! Turn left at the next street," Mike said suddenly.

"What? Why?"

"Just turn."

Beth turned left and asked, "Where are we going?"

"I just remembered that steak dinner I promised you."

"I believe it was steak and lobster."

"I know a good steakhouse up the road here, but I don't think they serve lobster. Sorry. We'll have to get lobster another day."

Beth smiled and said, "Well, if I have to, I guess I could settle for a plain old boring steak dinner."

"It won't be boring because I will be with you."

"That sounds like a treat too good to pass up."

Mike looked at Beth and said, "I can't tell. Are you serious or being sarcastic?"

"Yes," Beth said.

Mike drove to the center of the business district and parked in front of a place called "The Pampered Cow." It was sandwiched between a pastry shop and an antique store.

"The Pampered Cow?" Beth said.

"Supposedly, the meat is better from cows that are well cared for and free from stress."

"I suppose they give them massages, too."

"Of course. You can't be a pampered cow without massages. I'm sure they also get pedicures. If I were to guess, though, I'd say they probably buy their meat from the same wholesaler as every other restaurant."

The place was relatively small, with only about ten tables. The hostess asked, "Do you have a reservation?"

"No, we don't," Mike said. "I was hoping you could squeeze us in."

The woman looked at her computer screen and said. "I have one table available near the kitchen. Is that okay?"

"We'll take it," Mike said.

The woman picked up a couple of menus and led them to a table near the back of the dining area. She put the menus on the table and said, "Your server will be with you shortly."

Beth looked at the menu and said, "Steak but no lobster. I'm giving you a C+."

Mike said, "That's disappointing. Is there anything I can do for extra credit?"

They were interrupted by a young woman who said, "Good evening. I'm Jenna. I'll be your server tonight. Would you like something to drink?"

"Beth said, "I'll have an unsweetened iced tea."

Mike said, "I'll have the same."

"Okay," The server said. "I'll put that in for you. Do you have any questions about the menu?"

"No, I think we're fine," Beth said.

When the server left, Mike asked, "You don't want a beer or a glass of wine?"

"No. I only drink on weekends."

"Really? Why is that?"

"When I was a teenager, I made a promise to myself that I would only drink alcohol on weekends."

"Today is Sunday. It's still technically the weekend."

"I don't consider Sunday evening the weekend."

"So why did you make that promise to yourself?"

"Because both of my parents were alcoholics. I saw what alcohol did to them, and I didn't want to go down that road."

"Oh, so you figured you could never get addicted if you had no alcohol five days a week."

"That was exactly what I thought, and it's worked so far."

"How are your parents now?"

My father died about five years ago. One night, he went out drinking with guys from work and wrapped his car around a tree."

"I'm so sorry," Mike said.

"Thanks. Some good did come from it. He didn't hurt anybody, but himself, and my mother hasn't touched a drop of alcohol since that day."

"Do you see your mom very often?"

"No, not really. She still lives in Florida. I made it down there last Christmas, but being a rookie, I don't get a lot of vacation time yet. I would like to visit her more often. She is a good person, especially now that she's sober. You know, just because I'm not drinking doesn't mean you can't order a beer."

"Well, actually, it does. I made a similar promise to myself when I was young," Mike said. "I promised I would never drink alone."

"Why did you make that promise?" Beth asked.

"Well, I think it was the first or second time I went to a bar with friends. I remember seeing several guys drinking alone at the bar. I remember feeling sorry for them and thought, 'I never want to be like that.'"

"Technically, you wouldn't be drinking alone because I'm here with you."

"You are right, and I could use that as a loophole, but I don't want to. To me, drinking alcohol is a social thing."

Their server showed up with their drinks and asked, "Have you decided what you would like?"

Beth ordered the filet mignon, and Mike ordered the prime rib. They handed their menus back to the server, and she left to put the order in.

"What about you?" Beth asked. "Do you see your parents much?"

"Unfortunately, I have not been home since I took this job, but I have a vacation planned for the middle of July. I wanted to return for the Fourth of July, but that is a busy time at the park, so I will go the following week instead."

"How was your childhood? Were your parents good to you when you were growing up?"

"I would give them an A+ for effort," Mike said. "We weren't exactly poor, but we had little extra money for luxuries, so I often went without things I wanted. Looking back, I realize I had two parents who loved me very much. It is something that many kids don't have."

Beth put her hand on his and said, "It looks like they raised a fine young man. I bet they are very proud."

Her touch aroused something in Mike. He wondered if the touch was a deliberate show of attraction or something more innocent than that. She removed her hand, and Mike said, "Thanks. I bet your mother is proud of you, too. I mean, having a daughter in the FBI is quite impressive. I'd have a bumper sticker saying, 'My child is making the world a safer place. What has your child done?'"

Beth laughed and said, "You are too funny. I don't think she has taken it that far yet."

"Maybe not," Mike said, "but surely she has told everyone she knows."

"I don't know. Maybe," Beth said, smiling.

"So, do you work out of the Washington office?"

"Yes. I have an apartment across the river in Alexandria."

"Do you like living there?"

"It's okay,"

"Just okay?"

"Honestly, I don't love it. It's just convenient. If I could live further away from the city, I would."

Their server arrived with their food and put it on the table. She said, "Is there anything else I can get for you?"

"No, thank you," Beth said.

When the server left, Mike said, "Life's too short to settle, Beth."

"That's easy for you to say. You live where you work and work in a beautiful place."

"That is a recent development that I had to work hard to achieve."

"Do you think I didn't work hard to get where I am?"

"No. Of course you did," Mike said. "I'm sorry. I didn't mean to upset you. It just seems like you have doubts about your career."

"No, I'm sorry. I shouldn't have snapped at you. I hate to admit it, but you are not wrong. Sometimes, I love my job, but other times, I am not so sure. I feel like I am a bystander in my own life. I'm just waiting for circumstances to make things either better or worse. It's as if I'm sitting on a fence and need something or someone to come along and push me one way or the other."

"I hope that something or someone comes along soon and pushes you in the best direction for you."

"Thank you, Mike. I hope so, too."

After dinner, Beth drove Mike back to his cabin. She leaned over and kissed him on the cheek. "Thank you for a nice dinner," She said. "I'll see you tomorrow."

Mike got out and walked to the cabin, thinking about the kiss. It was on the cheek, not the lips. What did that mean? Was it a prelude to something more, or did she just put him in the friend zone? When he went inside, Dave was still up and said with a big grin, "So, I see you've been putting in some overtime with that pretty FBI agent."

"Are you jealous?" Mike asked.

"No. I already have a pretty girlfriend. I'm happy for you. I was worried that your last girlfriend might have ruined you for every other woman."

"Don't worry about me. I'm fine."

"I'm sure you are, Buddy. So, did you get some?"

"What's wrong with you? We are just working together temporarily."

"I guess that means you struck out, huh? Well, there's always tomorrow."

"I don't think so. I think her last boyfriend ruined her for every other man. She just broke up with him, and it sounds like she's given up on men."

"That's normal after a breakup. It will pass. After all, a tiger can't change its stripes."

"She also lives too far away. The best I could hope for is a one-night stand."

"That's way better than a zero-night stand."

"You have a good point. What would you do if you were me?"

"If I were you, I would get a haircut. Other than that, just be yourself. You're a nice guy who can be tough when he needs to be. As far as women are concerned, you are in the Goldilocks Zone."

Chapter 6

Beth was awakened in the middle of the night by a knock on the door. When she opened it, she saw Mike standing there. "I couldn't sleep," he said. "I need something from you."

"You do? What do you need?" Beth asked.

"This," he said, and leaned over and kissed her. She kissed him back, and it quickly became uncontrollable. Mike unbuttoned her shirt and removed it. He looked her up and down and said, "You are so beautiful."

They kissed some more while Beth unbuttoned Mike's shirt and took it off. He was in fantastic shape. He put his arms around her and pulled her close just as her phone started to ring. "Don't answer it," he said.

"I have to. It might be my boss."

Beth reached for her phone and suddenly realized where she was. She was alone in her cabin. Daylight shone through the windows. "Damn," she thought as she answered the phone.

"Good morning, Beth. It's Mike. There's an emergency meeting in one hour. Do you want to come?"

Beth looked at the clock next to the bed. It was almost seven o'clock. "Okay, she said. I'll be ready in forty-five minutes."

"Okay, I'll pick you up then," Mike said.

Beth took a shower and was getting ready when her phone rang again. It was Beth's supervisor, Robert Klein. She considered ignoring the call, but eventually answered. "Good morning, sir."

"Good morning, Miss Hartley. Do you have anything to report regarding the Drake kidnappers?"

Beth was okay with stretching the truth, but she didn't want to lie, so she said, "It appears there were no kidnappers, sir. There is, however, something strange going on around here, and I'd like to stay and try to figure out what it is."

"Strange? In what way?"

"Well, besides the Drake incident, there was a meteorite strike and a bear attack. Also, Emma's friends both died from suspicious causes. In addition, there is an emergency meeting this morning at the park. I can only assume something else bad has happened. I want to find out one way or another if this might be a biological attack."

There were several seconds of silence, and Klein said, "Okay. This was supposed to be your time off, so I'll let you be the judge. Stay on it for now, but keep me informed. I need to give this information to the director and see what he thinks."

"Okay. Thank you, sir."

She finished getting ready two minutes before Mike showed up to pick her up. When she opened the door, Mike looked at her and said, "Wow! You look great.

"You sound surprised."

"Well, I'm used to women who need an hour and a half to get ready."

"I'm not most women,"

"Clearly."

"So, what's the meeting about?"

"I don't know," Mike said. "We'll find out soon enough."

The meeting was held outside, not far from the visitor's center. About two dozen rangers, a dozen sheriff's deputies, and several other park employees stood outside while Superintendent Johnson addressed the crowd. "As most of you know, we have had more than our share of tragedies these last few days. There was the death of two young hikers as well as a deadly bear attack on one of our campers."

There was a hushed noise coming from the crowd as Johnson continued. "I just learned this morning that a couple of hikers found a young university student on the trail yesterday evening. He suffered an apparent heart attack but was still alive. He was taken to the hospital, but we have no further information on his condition at this time."

Mike looked at Beth and asked, "Are you thinking what I'm thinking?"

Beth just nodded as Johnson continued. "Furthermore, I also learned this morning that the cause of death of the bear that attacked the camper was a cerebral aneurysm, which is the same thing that killed the two young hikers. Ranger Mike here, and Agent Hartley from the FBI have theorized that the recent meteorite strike could be toxic. People are coming from the Environmental Protection Agency to make that determination. In the meantime, we are closing everything within a three-mile radius of where the incidents took place. We need to clear people out of the area as soon as possible. The sheriff's office has agreed to help. They will close Skyline Drive, and we will close the trail. We will reopen once we learn what is happening and determine it is safe. Are there any questions?"

Mike raised his hand and said, "We ran into a professor from the university yesterday. He had a student with him. If this student is the same person, perhaps the professor is still out there."

"If that is true, then that is a problem," Johnson said. "I can't risk sending a search party into the woods if there is something toxic out there. I will inform the EPA when we finish here. Does anyone else have a question?" After a silent pause, he said, "Okay, you all know what to do."

When the crowd began to disperse, Johnson walked over to Mike and Beth. He said, "Agent Hartley, are you staying for this? It seems you already found what you are looking for."

"Yes, sir," Beth said. "I can't be sure this toxin isn't manufactured. It could be someone is practicing for a much bigger attack."

He looked at her momentarily and asked, "Do you believe that, or is that an excuse to remain here to satisfy your curiosity?"

Beth smiled and said, "Does it matter what I believe?"

"Well, since you're staying, perhaps you two would like to return to the hospital and see what this young man knows. Maybe he can lead us to that meteorite."

"That's a great idea," Beth said.

"I agree. We'll let you know as soon as we learn something," Mike said.

When they got in Mike's vehicle, Beth said, "Take me to my car. I'll drive."

"Fine," Mike said. "I can get used to having a chauffeur."

"Enjoy it while you can. It's not often you get rewarded for doing a bad job."

"Really? You must not follow politics."

Beth laughed and said, "Okay, you have a point, but outside of politics and government, people don't usually get rewarded for doing a bad job, so consider yourself lucky."

After they changed cars and were on the way to the hospital, Mike asked, "That stuff you said earlier about this being a possible attack, do you believe that, or was Johnson right about you just wanting to satisfy your curiosity? Or maybe you want to spend more time with me."

"That girl who used to think she needed a man in her life no longer exists, so you can get that idea out of your head. As far as this being some kind of terrorist attack, I believe it is a possibility, and I think it's important to at least look into it, just in case. If you want to know if I truly believe it, I think it's unlikely, but I've been wrong before. I guess mostly I want to satisfy my curiosity."

"Wait a minute. Let's go back to the part about you being wrong. Did that really happen?"

"You really are quite the comedian, Mike."

"So, I take it you like mysteries."

"Of course. Who doesn't? Solving mysteries is one of the things that attracted me to this job."

"What was the most satisfying case that you worked on?"

"I've only been on the job a short time, but two months ago, we busted a human trafficking operation that was bringing young women into this country and forcing them prostitution. Freeing those girls and putting the assholes responsible behind bars was very satisfying."

"I imagine it was," Mike said. "You must have been like a hero to them."

"I think we were. It was a great feeling."

"What was your worst case?"

"The worst? Wow, I don't know. We never solved a couple of cases, which was disappointing, but I think the worst was when we were tasked with digging up dirt on a federal judge. He was supposedly suspected of taking bribes from organized crime, but things didn't add up. His conviction rate was about what you would expect. There was one high-profile case where the defendant walked, but I looked at that case and thought it was more likely the prosecutor was on the take."

"So, you think it was a political witch hunt?"

"I think it was. It turns out we did find dirt on the judge, but not what we expected. He was cheating on his wife with a prosecutor from one of his recent cases. She lost that case, but it didn't matter. He was removed from the bench and replaced by another judge just before the trial of a senator's son accused of taking a minor across state lines for sex or something like that. The son was cleared of all charges. Of course, that might have all been a coincidence. I don't know."

"I guess it's like any other job. You have to take the good with the bad."

"I suppose so," Beth said. "What about you? You never told me about your time in the Army."

"That's because there's not much to tell."

"C'mon. I told you my stories. It's your turn. What was your best case?"

After a momentary hesitation, Mike finally said, "Okay, fine. My best case wasn't a case at all. I was stationed near Stuttgart, Germany. I was in town one night with a couple of my men. We just went out for a beer. As we were finishing up and getting ready to leave, I noticed a group of privates at a table on the other side of the bar. They were all acting a little rowdy, possibly because of the pretty waitress taking their order. As she left, one of the men grabbed her ass."

Beth said, "I think I know where this is going."

"I'm sure you do," Mike said. "Anyway, I grabbed the man by his collar and dragged him outside. I gave him probably the best speech I have ever given in my life. I wish I could remember my exact words. I said we were there representing the United States of America. I said it is a country that deserves respect, but nobody in that bar will respect America after watching his behavior that night. I then made him apologize to the waitress, and I think he meant it."

Beth put her hand on Mike's knee and said, "That might seem minor, but I bet that man never disrespected women after that."

"I don't know if you can change people that easily, but I do hope I had some influence on his future behavior."

"I think you did," Beth said. "What about the worst? What's the worst thing that happened over there?"

Mike slowly shook his head and said, "I can't think of anything."

"Surely it couldn't have been all good," Beth said.

There was a moment of silence, and then Mike said, "Can we change the subject?"

Clearly, something bad happened, Beth thought, but she didn't want to upset him further, so she said, "Sure. What about pretzels? I hear they are very good over there."

***

When Mike and Beth arrived at the hospital, a helpful volunteer directed them to room 208 on the second floor. They found James Black alone in his room, sitting up and watching a game show on the television. He had a large bandage on his forehead and another on his right arm. When he saw them come in, he turned the television off and said, "I saw you two yesterday on the trail, didn't I?"

"That's right," Beth said. "I'm Agent Hartley with the FBI, and this is Ranger Mike. We are here to learn what happened to you in the woods, Mr. Black."

"Please, call me James."

"Okay, James," Beth said. "What happened out there yesterday?"

"Well, after we saw you two, Professor Brown and I ventured into the woods to find that meteorite. It took a long time, but we eventually found it. It was too big to take back with us, so we chipped off a few pieces and started heading back to the trail. On the way, I started feeling weird."

"Weird? How so?" Mike asked.

I'm not sure how to describe it. I felt anxious but not frightened. It was more like I was pumped up and ready to go into battle. It was odd because there was no reason to feel that way. Then, an argument started between Professor Brown and me. It was stupid, really. I liked him, but he was acting like a dick all of a sudden. It was totally out of character for him, and it made me angrier than I had ever been in my life, at least that I can remember. We started fighting. In the middle of the fight, he started talking gibberish, like he was having a stroke. Before that, it felt like the primitive part of my brain had taken over, but seeing Professor Brown have a stroke brought me back to reality."

"What happened to Doctor Brown?" Beth asked.

James paused, searching for the right words, and finally said, "He didn't make it. When it happened, my head started hurting, and then my heart beat so fast that it felt like my chest would explode. I lay on the ground, hoping it would slow down, but I was almost certain I would die there. I must have blacked out because it was almost sunset when I came to. I checked on the professor, but he was gone by then. I struggled to get myself back to the trail. It took a while, but I made it and blacked out again. The next thing I knew, I was here. Someone told me a couple of hikers found me."

"You are lucky to be alive," Mike said.

"So, what do you two know about this?" James asked.

"We were hoping you could tell us," Mike said. "I can only tell you that two other people and a bear were also affected."

"How are they doing?" James asked.

Mike looked at Beth and then back at James. "I'm afraid none of them made it."

James looked out the window for several seconds and said, "So what does that mean for me? Am I going to die?"

"Not likely," Beth said. "We're not doctors, but you made it through the worst of it and are still here. You must have a strong heart or something."

"I guess playing basketball twice a week paid off."

"I'm sure it didn't hurt," Mike said. "We just have a couple more questions for you, and then we'll let you rest. Where can we find Doctor Brown, and where is the meteorite?"

"Find out where those hikers found me on the trail and then go southeast for about a half mile. Look for trees with broken tops. They will lead you to the meteorite. Professor

Brown is about halfway between the meteorite and the trail. Maybe a little closer to the trail."

"Thanks so much," Mike said.

They found the doctor in charge of his care after they left his room. Beth thought she was young and pretty, perhaps too young and too pretty. How could she possibly know what she was doing? Then she realized that is what many people thought of her. She showed the doctor her identification and said, "Hi. I'm Agent Beth Hartley, and this is Ranger Mike Bauer. Can we ask you a few questions about James Black?"

"I'm sorry, but I'm afraid I can't give out medical information about my patient."

Beth hadn't considered that and knew arguing would be pointless. "What if he gives you permission?"

"Well, I suppose that would be okay."

"Good," Beth said, and they walked back to James's room. When they got there, Beth asked, "James, will you please give the doctor permission to talk to us about your condition?"

"Of course," he said, "but I want to hear this too."

"Well, Mr. Black suffered a myocardial infarction. A heart attack. We are waiting for the lab reports before we know more," the doctor said.

"Three people and a bear have died mysteriously, including Mr. Black's companion," Beth said. "The county coroner told us two of the deaths were caused by an aneurysm, which was the result of an overwhelming amount of adrenaline caused by some unknown substance. Could that have also caused Mr. Black's heart attack?"

"That is about the best explanation I can think of. I couldn't understand why someone as seemingly healthy as Mr.

Black here would suffer a heart attack. There are no other signs of heart or vascular issues. Even his blood pressure is below average."

"So, what could he have been exposed to that would spike his adrenaline?" Beth asked.

I'm afraid I have never seen anyone's adrenaline increase that much through toxic exposure. Some drugs can increase adrenal production, but not to levels that would cause a heart attack. Plus, he would have to ingest it. An airborne contaminant that could do that is beyond my area of expertise."

"Well, thank you, doctor," Beth said. "We won't take up any more of your time." To James, she said, "We appreciate you talking with us, James, and wish you the best."

When they stepped outside, Mike called Superintendent Johnson and told him where to look for the meteorite and the body of Doctor Brown.

They then headed back to the park. Once they were on the way, Mike said, "We didn't learn much, but it seems less likely that this was a terrorist attack."

"I never really believed that," Beth said, "but, at the same time, nothing disproves it either."

"Those two men literally chipped off pieces of that meteorite, and now one is dead, and another is in the hospital."

"I know," Beth said. "That rock is looking like the most likely cause. The problem is, once someone determines that the meteorite is toxic, I will be sent back to Washington, and I am starting to like being out here in nature."

"I know exactly how you feel, Beth, but if you want to be an FBI agent, you have to do FBI stuff."

Beth laughed and said, "Oh, is that how it works? Thanks for letting me know."

"My pleasure. Let me know if there's anything else I can do to help."

***

When they returned to the park, they switched vehicles and headed to the visitor's center. Two vans from the EPA were there. There was also a van from the coroner's office with two men sitting inside. Presumably, they expected to recover Doctor Brown's body. Next to the coroner's van was an ambulance. They weren't taking any chances. Eight people from the EPA, six men and two women, were all there putting protective clothing over their street clothes. They carried masks hooked up to a portable oxygen machine. Mike's roommate, Dave, was part of the group, bringing the number up to nine. When Mike got close, he said, "I see they roped you into the dangerous work."

"I volunteered," Dave said. "Someone needs to lead these people. Besides, I've never seen a meteorite before. This is something I can tell my grandchildren about."

"Grandchildren? You don't even have kids."

"Not yet, but I'm still young."

"Well, if you want to have kids, be careful out there."

Dave put his hand over his heart and said, "Your concern is touching." He then let out a big laugh.

"Just be careful," Mike said. "If you die, I'll have to make my own coffee."

"I guess I'll have to be careful then. I wouldn't want you to suffer like that."

Mike patted Dave on the shoulder and said, "I'll see you later, buddy." He then walked with Beth to Superintendent Johnson's office.

"Mike. Agent Hartley," Johnson said. "Thanks for getting that information to us. We should have that damn rock located and removed before the day is out. Then we can get back to normal."

"That would be nice, sir."

"Most of the guests should be out of the area by now. I need you to help check for stragglers."

"Will do," Mike said. He turned to Beth and asked, "Do you want to come, or should I take you back to your cabin?"

"No. I'll ride with you."

They got in Mike's SUV and drove for several minutes, not seeing a soul except two other rangers. The area seemed empty of people, but as they drove past a camping area, they spotted a pickup truck and a lone tent. Mike drove toward the tent and saw two men sitting on lawn chairs in front of it. They were each holding a beer.

Mike and Beth got out and approached the men. "Hello, gentlemen," Mike said.

Both men were in their early thirties. They both had full beards and wore flannel shirts. The man on the left was of average size. He wore a baseball cap with a picture of a dog and the word "Mack" under the dog. The other man wore no hat. He was much bigger. Part of the extra bulk was muscle, but he was also overweight. He said, "Hi, Ranger. Hi, Ma'am."

"I'm sure you're aware everyone was ordered to leave," Mike said. "Why are you two still here?"

The big man said, "We drove six hours to be here and then spent another hour setting up camp. Now you want us to pack up and leave. No, thank you."

"It's not a request, and it's for your own good. There are other campsites available north of here."

The big man stood up. He stood at least five inches taller than Mike, and Mike was six feet tall. He said, "We're not leaving."

Mike looked at Beth, who pulled out her identification and said, "FBI! You men need to leave now, or you'll find yourself in jail. I'm sure you don't want that."

The big man laughed, put his hands forward, and said, "Are you gonna handcuff me, pretty lady? I might like that."

Beth took out her gun and pointed it at the man, who just laughed at her. "Are you gonna shoot me, pretty lady? I bet that will go over well with your boss. You can tell him you shot me to protect me." He laughed again.

The smaller man spoke up and said, "Maybe we should just leave, Earl."

"Don't be a pussy, Jesse," the man said. "We're not gonna let these government people tell us what to do."

"Okay. Enough is enough," Mike said. He got out his radio, gave their location, and said, "We have a couple of men here refusing to leave. We need some backup and a tow truck to remove their pickup truck."

An angry look came over the big man's face. He said, "Ain't nobody touching my truck."

"Mike looked the big man in the eyes and said, "You men and your truck are on government property. As a duly appointed government representative, I have the authority to remove both you and your truck. I think I'll start with the truck."

"The hell you will," the big man said just before attempting to punch Mike in the face.

Mike ducked under the punch, delivering a hard blow to the man's solar plexus. The man bent over, gasping for air. Mike grabbed his left hand and twisted it behind his body. He held it with his left hand while he grabbed the man's collar with his right hand. He then pushed the man forward hard until he lost his balance. He fell forward, breaking his fall with his right hand, which Mike grabbed and pulled behind his back. He took handcuffs from his back pocket and clipped them to the man's wrist.

Mike stood up, looked at the other man, who raised his hands, and said, "We don't want any trouble. We'll leave. It's no problem."

Beth looked at Mike and said, "That was amazing. I'm sorry I doubted you."

"Well, he wasn't an Army Ranger."

"Still impressive," Beth said.

"Thanks."

"I'm just surprised you carry handcuffs."

Mike reached into his pocket and pulled out a small container. "I have pepper spray, too. You never know what kind of people you will encounter in this job."

"Maybe you should have used that."

"I'll remember that next time someone surprises me with a punch to the face."

They waited for backup to arrive and put the big man in the back of one of the vehicles while the smaller man packed the tent. They then let the big man go under the condition that they both leave the park and not come back. They didn't have the time or manpower to deal with prisoners, and both men were suddenly agreeable to leaving.

Chapter 7

Dave Vargas and the team of scientists got in the vans and drove as close as they could to the spot where James Black was found. They brought along a large wagon that held a special airtight metal box. They expected to recover the meteorite and needed a way to safely transport it in case it was as toxic as expected. Dave thought it looked like a coffin.

When they reached the correct location on the trail, the wagon needed to be left behind because traveling through the uncut forest was difficult for people alone. Pulling a wagon through the forest was virtually impossible.

After everyone put on their masks, Dave led the group into the woods. He felt comfortable there. The forest was in his blood. He was literally born inside a national park. His father was a Mexican guardaparque, similar to an American park ranger. Since he spoke English well, he and a few other guardparques came to America for a two-week cultural exchange program with the U.S. Park Service. American park rangers went to Mexico during that same time. Dave's father brought his pregnant wife with him for the two-week trip. She wasn't due for a month, but she went into labor prematurely and had the baby inside the park.

Since Dave was born in the United States, he was automatically a U.S. Citizen. Because of that, he became fascinated with America. He practiced English whenever he could, and after finishing school, he moved to Texas to study forestry at a state college there. He paid for his education with some money his parents saved up for him, but mostly, he worked his way through college as a waiter in a high-end seafood restaurant. When he started, he knew little about seafood, but he did know how to talk to people, especially women who tipped him very well.

After about ten minutes of walking, someone spotted something in the distance. When they got close, they saw it was Doctor Brown. Expecting they would find his body, they brought along a body bag. They put the body into the bag and zipped it closed. Dave did not want to split the group up, so they took the body back to the coroner's van together and continued back through the forest.

After they passed the point where Doctor Brown was found, they passed an area devoid of tall trees. It seemed to run in a general north-south direction, like it was a road at one time, but nature had reclaimed it, especially to the north, where the clearing abruptly ended. From that small clearing, Dave spotted the broken treetops in the distance. They continued in that direction until they came upon the meteorite.

The leader of the group was a middle-aged woman named Dr. Catherine Blake. When she saw the meteorite, she said, "It's hard to believe this little thing could cause so much death."

"Little? Dave said. "I bet it weighs three hundred pounds."

"It's all relative," Doctor Blake said.

"Let's see how relative it is as we carry it back."

Doctor Blake put a glove on it and said, "It's amazing, isn't it?"

"Amazing?" Dave said. "What do you mean?"

"I mean, just a few days ago, this thing was hurtling through space at a speed we can't even imagine. Now it is here waiting for us to take it away."

"It is amazing if you think of it like that," Dave said, "but I expected it to look more interesting. I mean, it just looks like a rock."

"Did you think it would have a green glow or something, like on television?"

"I don't know what I expected," Dave said. "I just thought it would look different."

They weren't there to analyze the meteorite on the spot. Their main objective was securing it and returning it to the lab. They had a tarp with them that they put on the ground next to the rock. Several of the men removed dirt from around the meteorite, rolled it onto the tarp, and then wrapped it. They also brought straps with them that movers sometimes use to help them lift heavy furniture. They slid three straps under the rock, and six men used the handles at the ends of each strap to pick the rock off the ground. They carried it through the woods, setting it down every hundred yards or so to rest. The way back was longer in distance because they had to take a zig-zag pattern to avoid clumps of trees that were too narrow for the group to fit through.

Dave and Doctor Blake led the group. Two coyotes appeared before them when they came close to where they found Doctor Brown. They both started growling and howling. Dave put his hand out and said, "Be still. Coyotes usually avoid humans unless they feel threatened or are protecting their young. Since we came through here already, I doubt they are protecting their young, so they should go away if we don't threaten them."

They all stood very still, but the coyotes continued to approach. Mike took out his can of pepper spray just as both coyotes ran towards them. He stepped in front of Doctor Blake and hit the lead animal in the face. It made a loud whining sound and fell to the ground. It got up and retreated, falling every few feet. The other coyote managed to get through and jumped onto Dave's chest. Dave lost his balance and fell to the ground. The coyote tried to bite his neck, but instead ripped his air hose in half. Catherine picked up the pepper spray that Dave dropped, pushed the coyote off him with her foot, and hit it in the face with the pepper spray. It, too, retreated like the first one.

Doctor Blake then knelt and examined Dave's wounds. His face and neck were scratched and bleeding. The animal also managed to get its claws through all the layers of clothing and into Dave's chest. She determined the wounds were not life-threatening, but exposure to the air near the meteorite might be lethal. She picked up Dave's radio and said, "This is Doctor Blake. We have a medical emergency. A coyote attacked Ranger Dave. It bit through his air hose and caused multiple lacerations. We're bringing him in."

She directed her group to wait until they were clear and then continue carrying the rock while she and the young woman from the group helped to get Dave to the waiting ambulance. He felt okay to walk, but Doctor Blake worried the excitement could speed up the coming adrenaline spike.

They made it back to the trail, where two paramedics and a couple of rangers waited with a stretcher. Dave didn't want to be carried, but Doctor Blake insisted that he exert himself as little as possible. When they got him to the ambulance, Mike and Beth were there waiting. They had heard the call for help, and Mike feared his friend would end up like the others. "How's he doing?" Mike asked when they got close.

"I'm fine," Dave said. "It's just a few scratches."

"You don't feel anxious or excited?" Mike asked.

"Not at all," he said. "They wrapped that rock in a tarp. That must have contained all its bad mojo."

Mike looked at the paramedics and asked, "Did you check his pulse?"

One of them said, "Yes. It's normal."

"Check it again," Mike said.

The paramedic put his fingers on Dave's wrist and looked at his watch. After several seconds, he said, "It's still normal."

"That's a relief," Mike said. "I was worried I'd have to make my own coffee."

Everyone laughed before Dave was loaded into the ambulance. "Don't worry about me," Mike said. "I can make my own coffee for a day, maybe two."

The two men closed the door and then drove away. Mike noticed the two women who followed Dave out of the woods. "What the hell happened out there? He asked.

Doctor Blake spoke up and said, "Ranger Dave risked his life to save us. Two coyotes attacked us, and he stepped in front of me and took the hit."

Beth asked, "Are you in charge here?"

"Yes, I am. I'm Doctor Catherine Blake." She shook hands with Beth and Mike.

Beth took out a business card and said, "Please call me as soon as you learn what is wrong with that rock."

Just then, they noticed the rest of the group come out of the woods, pulling the cart with the meteorite encased in its metal coffin. Doctor Blake said, "I have to go, but I will let you know."

She met up with her group as they loaded the container into one of the vans. They then folded the cart and slid it next to the container. Mike and Beth watched as they piled into the two vans and drove away.

"There go all our problems," Mike said.

"Don't jinx it," Beth said.

"Oh, don't tell me you're superstitious."

"I am not superstitious. I'm just not arrogant enough to think that all my beliefs are one hundred percent correct."

"That's good. Having an open mind seems necessary for someone in your profession."

"You would think," Beth said, "but it seems many of my colleagues are wedded to their beliefs. I think human nature is quite complex. We all want to be right, so we believe people who think like us and disbelieve people who think differently."

"You are too young to be this wise."

Beth smiled and said, "You are quite the smooth talker."

"Only because I've been hanging around Dave too long."

"Well, Mr. Dave Wannabe, don't you think it's time we eat something? I'm hungry."

"You are reading my mind, young lady," Mike said. "How do you feel about hamburgers?"

"I like hamburgers if they are made right. Do you know a good place to get burgers around here?"

"I sure do," Mike said. "My place."

"Your place? You mean the guy who can't make coffee is going to make us hamburgers?"

"I can make coffee just fine. Dave just happens to be more of a morning person than I am."

"Okay, Mike. Let's go. Show me what you can do."

***

They drove to Mike's cabin. When they arrived, Mike took out everything he needed. He formed two hamburger patties and put them in a pan on the stove. He then sliced a tomato while the burgers were cooking. When they were almost finished, he topped them with a slice of cheese. He took out two buns, added mayonnaise to the bottom of each one, and placed the hamburgers on top. He then added the tomatoes and lettuce before putting the top on.

Beth sat at the small kitchen table and watched Mike cook. When finished, he brought the burgers to the table and sat across from her. Beth took a bite of her burger but didn't say anything.

"Well?" Mike asked.

"Well, what?"

"Do you like it?"

"It's acceptable."

"Acceptable? Really?"

Beth smiled and said, "If you really need positive reinforcement, then yes, I like it. It is the best hamburger I have ever had in my life."

"Are you like this with everyone, or am I special?"

"You are special," Beth said before taking another bite of her hamburger.

"I can see why you don't have a boyfriend," Mike said.

Mike drove Beth back to her cabin when they finished eating the pizza. She kissed him once and got out. Before she closed the door, she said, "I enjoyed our time together. I will see you before I leave tomorrow."

"I look forward to it," Mike said.

When Beth entered her cabin, she found a contact in her phone and dialed the number. "Hey, it's Beth," she said. "I need everything you can find on a Michael Bauer. He's a park ranger at Shenandoah National Park. Thanks."

Chapter 8

Beth woke up early the following morning and checked her messages. The report on Ranger Mike was waiting for her. She read it carefully and then put her phone down and thought.

She took a shower and started to put her makeup on when her phone rang. The phone number appeared on her phone without a name. She answered it. "This is Agent Hartley."

"Agent Hartley. Hi. This is Catherine Blake from the EPA. You told me to call you when we learned something."

"Yes, Doctor Blake. What did you find?"

"Well, you won't like it, but we found nothing unusual about the meteorite. It's perfectly harmless."

"What? That can't be. Are you sure?"

"We did every test we could think of. It turns out it's just like any other rock."

"That doesn't make any sense. What happened to all those people?"

"We want to know that just as much as you do, Agent Hartley. We are preparing another team to go down there tomorrow morning."

"Why not today?" Beth asked.

"We wouldn't be able to get there until late afternoon, and you are expected to get some heavy rain there by then. There wouldn't be much we could do."

"Okay, Doctor Blake. Thanks for letting me know."

Beth finished getting ready and then called her supervisor. She told him the meteorite was clean and asked what he wanted her to do. "I already know they found nothing in that meteorite," Klein said. "The director got a call from Senator Drake. He knew before we did. He wants us to stay on it. He's worried that whatever is in the air out there might have a long-term effect on his daughter, and he wants answers. So, stay there. Work with the EPA if you must, but find out what the hell is going on out there."

"Yes, sir," Beth said. "I'll do what I can."

She didn't bother calling Mike. She just got in her car and drove to his cabin. She knocked on the door and waited. After a minute, she knocked again. The door finally opened, and Mike stood there naked except for a towel wrapped around his waist. His hair was wet, and he had a surprised look on his face. "Beth. I didn't expect you to be ready so early. Come on in. Give me a few minutes to finish getting ready."

"Take your time," she said as Mike disappeared into the bathroom. Beth thought about following him into the bathroom and taking him right there. He could lean her against the sink. No! Banish the thought. She could watch him in the mirror. No! She couldn't let herself fall for this guy, no matter how good-looking he was. She had her own life and didn't need any complications right now.

"So, why are you here so early?" Mike asked from the bathroom.

Beth didn't feel like explaining everything to him from another room. "I'll tell you when you are done in there."

"I'll be just a minute," he said as he left the bathroom, still wearing just a towel, and went into the bedroom.

"I'll be here," Beth said.

Three minutes later, he came out mostly dressed, except his shirt was unbuttoned. As he was buttoning it, he looked at Beth and said, "What did you want to tell me?"

Beth had the urge to unbutton his shirt, but stood her ground and said, "All of the tests on the rock came back negative. Whatever has been causing all these problems has nothing to do with that meteorite."

"I heard the news before you got here," Mike said.

Beth looked surprised and said, "You did? From whom?"

"The superintendent called about ten minutes ago. He got a call from Senator Drake, who is eager to find out what is going on. He wants me to continue working with you until we solve this mystery."

"My boss got the same call. It seems the good senator wants both of us on the case. He wants to ensure his daughter has not been exposed to anything that might affect her health in the future. So, I guess we're stuck with each other for a little longer."

"It's been a while since I had a partner," Mike said. "Professionally, I mean."

"I sometimes work with a partner, but it is not always the same person," Beth said.

"That's surprising," Mike said. "How do you build trust if your partner constantly changes?"

"It's not like I have someone different every single time, but often, they give the assignments to whoever has the right gifts for the situation. If we want to take down a white-collar criminal, someone who can hack computers works better than someone good at negotiating with kidnappers."

"I see your point, but I would still rather have someone that I know well and who knows me well. It is much easier to work as a team that way."

"I'm surprised to hear you say that, Mike, considering one of your own men betrayed your trust."

Mike looked shocked at the statement and said, "You had me checked out. Why would you do that?"

"I needed to know if I could trust you to have my back. I worry because you left the military and became a park ranger because you could no longer trust the people you worked with. At least here, you can be on your own most of the time. I need to be able to trust you, and I need you to trust me."

"You check me out behind my back, and now you think I should trust you? Do they not teach you logic in the FBI? What about cause and effect?"

"I'm not sure why you are so angry. Doing a background check on someone is common and perfectly normal."

"Maybe in your world, it is. In my world, we respect people's privacy. Never mind the fact that you can't learn everything about a person from a report. If you must know, it is true that one of the men under my command betrayed my unit. He took bribes to look the other way, as several million dollars' worth of military equipment was stolen and sold on the black market. It is also true that I never fully trusted the guy. He seemed shady to me the moment he transferred to my unit. That is why I caught him. You, on the other hand, I thought I could trust. I guess we all make mistakes. You should leave now. Talk to the superintendent. Tell him you want a new partner."

Mike's reaction stunned Beth, and she suddenly felt as though she had made a grave error, one from which she could not recover. She left the cabin and got into her car. She sat there for a long while but didn't start the engine. She tried to hold back the tears, but she wasn't strong enough. She screwed up big time. How could she fix it? She knew an apology would not work, but she had to start there. She got out of her car and knocked on Mike's door. She waited thirty seconds and knocked again. Finally, the door opened. Mike looked at her but said nothing.

"Can I come in?" Beth asked.

Mike hesitated for a few seconds and then opened the door all the way and stepped aside.

Beth walked in, closed the door, and said, "I am so, so sorry. I did a terrible thing. I didn't consider your feelings, and I am ashamed of that. I have become so accustomed to allowing a computer to make judgments that I should be making myself. Will you forgive me?"

Mike was quiet for several seconds and finally said, "I always believed people who are genuinely sorry deserve a second chance. I don't, however, believe in third chances."

"I agree," Beth said. "If I ever need a third chance, I won't deserve it."

"If we are going to work together, I need to know that you will be there when I need you, and you need to know the same thing about me. If we can't trust each other, you will be better off with someone else. That means no secrets. You tell me everything, and I will tell you everything. Can you do that?"

"I can do that," Beth said. "I trust you and promise never to do anything behind your back again."

Mike studied her face for a moment as if looking for sincerity, then said, "I forgive you, but expect me to be angry for a while yet."

"I can live with that."

"Would you like something to eat before we head out?" Mike asked. "I don't have much left. I need to go shopping, but some frozen waffles are in the freezer."

"I like waffles," Beth said.

"Well, you might change your mind after you try these."

Mike took the box out of the freezer and took out four waffles. He had a four-slice toaster, so he was able to toast them all at once. While waiting for the toaster, he got out plates, silverware, and maple syrup. He made coffee before Beth arrived and poured two cups.

They didn't talk much during breakfast. When they finished, Beth helped clean up and asked, "So what should we do first today?"

"Dave is being released at noon, and we are going to pick him up. Before that, I thought we could do my normal patrol. We shouldn't see anyone, but you never know."

"I'm happy your friend is okay," Beth said.

"Yeah, he was lucky."

"Do you think we need to worry about being exposed to whatever is out there?"

"I think we do, but as long as we stick to the roads, we should be okay. If you are worried, I could go without you."

"No," Beth said immediately. "I'm not worried."

"Okay, then. We should get going."

Mike grabbed a bag that he had put Dave's clothes in earlier, and they got in his SUV.

***

Mike drove slowly as they wound their way through the forest. "This is beautiful out here," Beth said. "So much nature."

Mike looked at her for a moment and said, "You've never really had a break from the city, have you? I mean, you grew up in one urban area and then moved to another urban area when you took the job with the FBI."

"I suppose that is true. I did drive through some pretty rural areas on the way to Washington."

"I don't think that is the same thing."

"I suppose not," Beth said.

"I grew up in a small town that was probably not too different from the town where you grew up in some ways," Mike said. "The streets were lined with houses. We had cable TV, internet, and all the normal stuff. There was a supermarket, a hardware store, and pretty much anything you would need. The major difference, I guess, would be that the next nearest town was ten miles away, and everything in between was either forest or farms. It wasn't uncommon for high school kids to go hunting before school."

"That's amazing. When I was young, I could barely wake up in time to get to school."

"I was the same way. I've never been a morning person."

"You get used to it if you have to," Beth said.

Suddenly, a loud bang came from the vehicle's roof, which startled Mike and Beth. Mike looked up and said, "What the hell was that?"

He slowed down seconds before something hit the road in front of them. He slammed on the brakes and got out. Beth got out, too, and they both looked at what fell out of the sky in front of them.

"It's a duck," Mike said.

They looked up and saw an entire flock of ducks falling to the ground. They jumped back into the vehicle as ducks slammed into the ground around them. When it was over, they got out and looked at the carnage.

"Holy shit!" Beth said. "I've never seen anything like that. It's like we're in some kind of horror movie."

"Yes, but this is no movie."

Mike knelt to examine the closest duck. "It has no apparent injuries except for hitting the ground. It wasn't shot."

Mike stood up and looked around. He saw more than two dozen ducks scattered about on both sides of the roadway. A couple were still alive, but barely.

"Whatever is out there, these ducks must have found it," Beth said.

Mike walked over to several of the ducks and examined their position. He was able to make a rough guess in which direction they came from. He took out his phone and opened the compass app. "I would guess they were coming from the south-southeast," he said. He then opened the map and took a screenshot of their location.

"Is that where the meteorite was?" Beth asked.

"I think so, but I'm not sure. This road winds around a lot. We can check the map later. Right now, I want to bring one of these birds with us." He picked up the nearest duck and put it in the back of the vehicle. "It will be close, but I think we have time to get it to the coroner's office and still make it to the hospital in time to pick up Dave. Let's find out if the coroner will autopsy a bird."

They got back in the vehicle, and Mike turned around and headed towards Roanoke. When they arrived at the coroner's office, Mike grabbed the duck, and they went inside. The woman behind the counter saw the duck and said, "Excuse me. You can't bring that in here."

Beth flashed her identification and said, "We need to speak with the medical examiner."

The woman hesitated and then went into the back. She returned a minute later with the medical examiner. It was the same doctor they had spoken with previously. "Good morning, Doctor," Mike said. "I know this is strange, but we need you to examine this duck and find out what killed it. We want to know if its death was caused by the same thing that killed those people the other day."

"I'm afraid I don't know anything about ducks. Perhaps a vet would be better able to help you."

"A vet hasn't seen what you saw in those people. You know what you are looking for."

The doctor sighed and held out his hand to take the duck. Mike handed it to him, and the doctor said, "I'll see what I can find."

"Thanks so much," Mike said.

Beth handed him her business card and said, "Please call me when you learn something."

***

They headed straight to the hospital when they left the coroner's office. They found Dave sitting in bed, waiting for the hospital to finish his paperwork so he could leave. He was still wearing his hospital gown and had a bandage on one side of his face. "How are you feeling, Buddy?" Mike asked.

"I'm fine. I was fine yesterday. I'm ready to get out of here."

Mike handed Dave the bag, and he said, "My clothes. Great. Thanks a lot. They didn't want me to put my bloody clothes back on."

"Yeah, that would probably not look good for the hospital if a patient left all bloody," Mike said.

Everyone laughed, and Dave went into the bathroom to change. Twenty minutes later, he was released, and they headed back to the park. Dave sat in the back seat and asked, "So, what did they learn about that meteorite?"

"It turns out it was harmless," Mike said.

"Seriously?" Dave asked.

"Yep. That's probably why you didn't get sick," Mike said. "Whatever is causing people to go crazy and die is still out there somewhere."

"That's unbelievable," Dave said. "What are the odds that people would go crazy after a meteorite strike, and the two are not related?"

Beth chimed in and said, "I'd say the odds are about one hundred percent."

Dave laughed and said, "So what do we do now?"

"There's no we," Mike said. "You have been ordered to take it easy for a few days."

"That's ridiculous," Dave said. "I'm fine."

"Maybe you are fine, Dave, but I was told to bring you home, and that's what I'm going to do. You can do what you want afterward, but Johnson wants you off duty until the doctor says otherwise."

Dave slumped back in his seat, and Beth said, "Do you have to bring him straight home? I'm getting hungry. Maybe we can stop for lunch first."

"That's a great idea, Beth," Dave said. "We are running low on food, and knowing Mike, he hasn't gone shopping yet."

"I've been kind of busy, you know," Mike said.

"Oh, yes. I'm sure you've been very busy," Dave said. "You need to remember that I won't always be here. You need to learn to do things on your own."

"What are you talking about? I do plenty. I just don't like shopping, but I do cook more than you do."

"Everybody has their strengths and weaknesses," Beth said, trying to break up the tension.

Mike looked back at Dave, and they both smiled. He then looked at Beth and said, "That's nice of you to intervene, but don't worry. We razz each other all the time."

"I should have known," Beth said. "Why do men give people they like a harder time than people they don't like?"

"I don't know," Dave said. "Maybe we are like kittens that pounce on each other for fun. It's like practice. When we need to insult somebody, we'll be ready."

"The ability to insult someone must have been a great survival tool for our hunter-gatherer ancestors," Beth said.

"Your sarcasm is noted, but I'm sure it was very helpful," Mike said. "Just think how many more people survived when two rival tribes fought each other with words instead of spears."

"I can't argue with that logic," Beth said.

They stopped at a local diner that Mike and Dave had visited many times. It started raining as they pulled into the parking lot, so they rushed inside. It was crowded. All the tables were taken, so they sat at the counter. An older woman wearing a name tag that read "Marie" approached them and said, "Hello, Ranger Mike. Hello, Ranger Dave. What happened to you?"

"Just a little scuffle with a coyote," Dave said.

"Oh, wow!" she said. "I never heard of them attacking humans before."

"It doesn't happen very often," Dave said. "I guess I'm special."

"You are special, Ranger Dave. I'm glad you're okay."

"Thanks, Marie."

"So, what can I get you today?"

Everyone gave Marie their order, and after she walked away, Dave said, "What do you think we should do the rest of the day?"

"You need to go home and rest," Mike said. "Doctor's orders. You need to let those wounds heal. You don't want to get an infection."

"What about you and me?" Beth asked. "We should do something."

"I'm not sure what we can do," Mike said. "The EPA won't be back until tomorrow. It's not like we can go traipsing through the woods unprotected. Besides, it's supposed to rain most of the day."

"I know, but it feels like we should be doing something. Sitting around at a time like this seems wrong."

"I agree. It does seem wrong. There's just nothing to do right now. Tomorrow will be a busy day, so perhaps rest would be the best thing for us today, too."

After lunch, they drove back to the park. They stopped first at Beth's cabin to drop her off. When she got out, Dave took her place in the front seat. Mike rolled his window down and said, "I'll call you in the morning. We'll probably leave early."

Beth stood in the rain, looking like she wanted to say something, but instead, she just nodded and went inside.

Once inside, Beth sat on the sofa, put her head back, and stared at the ceiling. She found the remote for the television and turned it on. She flipped through the channels for a few minutes and, seeing nothing worth watching, turned it off.

She sat there, thinking for a while, then picked up her phone and called her mother. "Hi, Honey," her mom said. "Are you just now getting home? You and, uh, John must have had a good time."

"I'm still here at the park, Mom."

"Oh, wow. How did you get the extra time off?"

"I didn't. I'm working on an assignment here."

"I'm confused, Beth. I thought you were there with John."

"It's a long story, but you were right about John. He was not the man for me."

"I'm sorry, Honey. Are you okay?"

There was a long pause while Beth gathered her thoughts. "I've been better, Mom. John never came. He blew me off for another woman."

"Oh, no. I'm so sorry, Honey. No wonder you are feeling bad."

"That's not even the worst of it. I don't even care about John anymore. I met a man. He's a park ranger here. I really like him, but I did something stupid, and now I fear he will never trust me again."

"That's a tough one, Honey. Trust is just as important as love in a relationship. You have two options right now. You can give up and forget about him, or prove that you are worthy of his trust. Which will you choose?"

"Thanks, Mom. You always have a way of making me feel better."

"That's what moms are for."

***

When Mike and Dave got to their cabin, Dave said, "That's quite a woman you got there. Why did you drop her off so early? She could have hung out here for a while."

"It's complicated," Mike said.

"Tell me. I have lots of experience with complicated."

"Well, she kind of pissed me off this morning. She let it slip that she ran a background check on me."

Dave looked perplexed and said, "So?"

"What do you mean, so? Don't you get it? She doesn't trust me."

"Trust you? She barely knows you. Wait a minute. She does know you. You slept with her, didn't you?"

Mike just nodded.

"You dirty dog. Now your feelings are hurt because you thought that it meant something."

"It did mean something," Mike said. "At least it did to me."

"Oh, so you think it didn't mean anything to her because she had you checked out. I think you are looking at it backward."

"Backward? How could I be looking at it backward?"

"Maybe she had you checked out because it did mean something to her. Maybe, consciously or even subconsciously, she considers you a good candidate for a future together. Maybe she's been burned before and wants to make sure you are not a wack job or something."

Mike thought for a moment and said, "You know, I hadn't thought of it that way."

"So now she's sitting in her cabin alone thinking you are some kind of an asshole."

"I have to admit it, Dave, but you're smarter than you look."

"And you are as funny as you look."

Mike grabbed his umbrella and opened the door to leave. He turned and said, "Don't wait up for me."

Dave gave him the thumbs up and said, "Go get her, buddy."

Mike drove to Beth's cabin and knocked on her door. She opened the door and looked surprised to see him. "Mike. What are you doing here?"

"May I come in?"

"Of course," Beth said as she moved aside to let him inside.

Mike stood by the door and said, "I may have overreacted this morning. I'm sorry. The truth is, you were mostly right. The man who betrayed my trust was more of a surprise to me than I let on. It is also partly true that I took this job because I felt I didn't need to rely as much on other people. Of course, being out in nature was also a big plus. Anyway, I just came here to tell you that."

"Beth looked at him momentarily and said, "You're not planning on leaving right away, are you?"

"Do you want me to stay?" Mike asked.

Beth put her hands on his face and kissed him passionately for several seconds before pulling away. "Does that answer your question?"

Mike kissed her back, and Beth started unbuttoning his shirt. "We need to get you out of these wet clothes."

Chapter 9

Mark Wesson was tired. It was a feeling he had often felt since his best friend had talked him into hiking the Appalachian Trail with him. He and Scott Ryan had been best friends since Scott moved in across the street when they were both seven years old.

Scott was the athletic one, excelling in every sport he ever became involved in. Mark was not athletic and always tended to be a bit overweight. He was, however, the smarter of the two. He excelled in math and planned on getting an engineering degree. Unfortunately, he was diagnosed with angina near the end of his first semester of college.

Mark took a semester off from school, and Scott decided that it was his responsibility as a best friend to help Mark get in shape. He tried to get Mark involved in various sports, but he just couldn't seem to motivate his friend. One day, he saw a news program about an elderly woman who had walked the entire Appalachian Trail, and he decided that was exactly what they needed to do. He figured Mark would have a hard time backing out once they were on the trail.

It took a while, but he finally convinced Mark that it would be an exciting adventure and the perfect thing to help Mark's health. They did their research, bought their supplies, and practiced. They set up and took down their tents dozens of times. They also filled their backpacks and walked around the block several times. They even slept in Mark's backyard for a couple of nights.

By early April, they were ready. Mark's parents drove them to Georgia and dropped them off at the start of the Appalachian Trail. It was rough going at first, and they made little progress, but gradually, they improved and covered slightly more distance each day.

Two months later, Mark was in much better shape but still tired after a long day of walking. That was perfectly normal. Scott was tired, too. They wanted to make it as far into Shenandoah as possible before camping for the night, so, despite the rain, they pushed themselves. By late afternoon, the rain gradually slowed and then stopped. The ground was wet, but it was a pleasant reprieve. Naturally, they were surprised when they came upon almost two dozen tents crammed close together, with many hikers just hanging around talking to each other. They asked one of them what was going on.

"The trail is closed," he said.

"What?" Scott said. "Why?"

"Not sure, exactly. Apparently, there is something toxic ahead."

"How long will it be closed?" Mark asked.

"No idea. Ask them," he said, pointing at a couple of rangers ahead on the trail.

They walked up to the rangers who were standing behind a temporary fence. "Hello, Rangers," Scott said. "Can you tell us how long the trail will be closed?"

One of them said, "We don't know. It could be open as early as tomorrow. It could be much longer."

"What's the problem?" Mark asked.

"Sorry," one of them said. "We don't know exactly. We just know there is a health risk out there."

Scott motioned for Mark to follow him and walked back past all the hikers. When they were far enough away, he said, "I don't want to sit around here for weeks. We will never complete the trail if we do that."

"What else can we do?" Mark asked.

"It's a national park. What could possibly be toxic? Poison ivy? Someone probably got bitten by an animal, and they are overreacting."

"You think so?" Mark asked.

"Yes. I'm sure of it."

"I don't know."

"Look, we've been walking for almost two months. Do you want to quit now after investing two months of your life into this? Don't you want to complete the trail? Imagine how many girls you could impress by telling them you walked the entire Appalachian Trail. We can't do that if we're stuck here."

Mark thought for quite a while and finally said, "Okay, what should we do?"

Scott looked both ways and then pointed to the right. "I think we can sneak through if we go that way."

"I don't know. It looks dense."

"Yes. Dense enough not to be seen but still passable, I think."

"Well, I guess we can try it," Mark said.

They walked back down the trail until they were out of sight of everyone and then made their way into the woods. When they were deep enough to ensure that nobody would see them, they came upon an area that looked like it had been cleared at one time. There were no tall trees in either direction, although there were small plants, shrubs, and a few small trees.

The clearing headed in a northerly direction. Since that was the way they wanted to go, they followed it for a half mile or so, then headed west through the trees again, back toward the trail.

By the time they reached the trail, the skies had cleared enough for them to see a beautiful sunset through the trees. They both looked around but saw nobody. "Piece of cake," Scott said. "Let's find a good place to pitch our tents."

They walked for less than ten minutes before finding a flat clearing that was perfect. They quickly set up their tents and then sat next to each other on a large log while digging through their packs for snacks. "This is pretty cool," Mark said as he unwrapped a granola bar. "I've never been much of a rebel before. It's kind of exhilarating."

"Yes, it is, my friend, but it's no big deal. It's not like we just robbed a bank or something. The worst that could happen is they make us leave."

A twig snapped behind them, and Mark turned and saw a flash of something knock Scott off the log. It took him a moment to realize what had happened. A large bobcat was on Scott's back, biting the side of his face. Mark jumped to his feet and instinctively backed away as the cat ripped part of Scott's ear off. Scott tried to get the animal off him, but lying on his belly was a precarious position.

Mark's instinct to survive was overruled by his desire to help his friend. He picked up his backpack, held it in front of his body, and charged the cat. He knocked the big cat off of Scott, but dropped the bag in doing so.

The cat hit the ground on its side but got to its feet before Mark could react. The cat used the backpack as a springboard and leaped at Mark, digging his claws into his chest and knocking him backward to the ground. He hit his head hard on the log and was knocked unconscious.

By then, Scott was on his feet, blood dripping down the right side of his face. He saw the cat on top of his friend, picked up the backpack, and threw it. It hit the cat on its hindquarters and caused it to yelp in pain. It then limped off into the woods.

Scott checked on his unconscious friend. His shirt was ripped, and he had blood coming from his chest and face. He looked around. He knew there was a road that sometimes ran parallel to the trail, but had no idea how close it was. He headed west into the woods and reached the road in less than ten minutes. He looked both ways but saw no cars. "Shit," he said out loud. Then, a light appeared in the distance. Scott watched as a car came around the corner. He stepped onto the road and waved his hands over his head.

***

After spending the rest of the afternoon in bed, Mike finally said, "Well, I suppose we should do something."

"I thought we were doing something," Beth said.

"You know what I mean. I feel a bit guilty that we haven't done any work this afternoon."

"You said yourself there was nothing we could do until tomorrow."

"I know. I just don't like idling."

"It looks like it stopped raining," Beth said. "Do you think there is anything we can do?"

"No, not really. Since this area is closed, we can only try to find the source of our problems, but we can't do that until tomorrow."

"So, you see? You have nothing to feel guilty about. Why don't we go out for dinner if you want to do something?"

"That's a good idea, but I'd rather cook something for you. Let's go to the store and pick up a few things."

"Sounds good to me," Beth said. "I'll never say no to a home-cooked meal, but I'm driving."

"Okay, driver," Mike said, smiling. "Bring the car around."

"Don't push your luck."

Beth's phone rang, but she didn't recognize the number. "Hello. This is Agent Hartley," she said.

"Hello, Agent Hartley. This is Doctor Reynolds, the county medical examiner."

"Hello, Doctor Reynolds, just a minute. I'm going to put you on speaker so my partner can hear." Beth hit the speaker button and held the phone out in front of her. "Okay. Go ahead."

"I got the cause of death from the duck you brought in," the doctor said. "It suffered a heart attack caused by too much adrenaline. The same cause as before. This duck had also been exposed to the same unknown chemical. What I found different was the amount of heavy metals in its system was lower, so I think we can conclude that whatever this unknown chemical is, it is the main cause of these ailments."

Beth and Mike looked at each other, and Beth said. "Thank you so much for that information, Doctor. You've been a big help."

After Beth hung up, Mike called the superintendent and told him about the ducks and the autopsy results. When he hung up, they got dressed and headed out.

When they got outside, they were treated to the remnants of a beautiful sunset. "For some reason, sunsets never look this good in the city," Beth said.

"Nothing looks this good in the city," Mike said.

Once they were on the road, Beth asked, "So, what are you planning on making for dinner?"

"I don't know," Mike said. "What do you like?"

"How about Italian food?"

"Oh, I love Italian food, and I make a pretty good tomato sauce, but that needs to cook for a while. Come to think of it, pretty much everything I know how to cook takes a while unless you want burgers again."

"No. Let's just go out for dinner tonight. I'll take a rain check on you cooking something."

Suddenly, a man stepped onto the street in front of them, waving his arms wildly. Beth stopped the car, and they both got out. The man was bleeding from his face, and it looked like part of his ear was missing. Mike grabbed his arms and looked at his ear, using the headlights for illumination. "What happened to you? Were you attacked?"

"A bobcat. It was a bobcat. It was crazy, like it had rabies or something. My friend is hurt badly. He needs help."

Mike looked at Beth and said, "The first aid kit is in my truck, along with my radio."

Beth took out her cell phone, looked at it for a moment, then said, "I have no signal."

"That's what I was afraid of," Mike said. "We don't have much choice. Let's see what we can do." He then turned to the man and said, "Where is your friend?"

The man pointed and said, "That way. He's near the trail."

"The trail is closed," Mike said. "What were you two doing out there?"

"We screwed up. Can we talk about that later?"

Mike looked at Beth and then back at the man. He said, "We'll go. You wait here."

"No way, man. He's my friend. I'm going too."

What's your name?" Beth asked.

"Scott," he said.

"Okay, Scott. Listen. You're hurt. If you were to pass out from blood loss or some other injury you may have, we would then have to carry two people out. That would really complicate things. Just wait here. You can sit in the car."

He hesitated but finally agreed. Beth opened the passenger door for him, removed her gun from the glove compartment, and tucked it into her pants. She was not wearing her holster. Mike looked at her, and she said, "If there is a wild animal out there, we need protection."

They made their way through the forest until they came upon the trail. They saw two tents in the distance and quickly walked in that direction. When they got close, they saw the young man lying on the ground. His chest was covered in blood, and the left side of his face was bleeding.

Mike put his ear against his mouth and said, "He's breathing. His head was next to a large log. Mike put his hand behind his head and felt a wound. He showed Beth the blood on his hand and said, "We need to get him to a hospital fast. I'm afraid we're going to get some blood on your seat."

"It's a government car," Beth said. "Is it safe to move him?"

"We'll have to risk it. Do you think you can help carry him?"

"I think so," Beth said. "I work out three times a week. I may be a girl, but I'm not weak."

"I do not doubt that," Mike said.

He put his hands under the man's arms while Beth carried his legs. It was slow going, and they had to stop and rest several times. It took about twenty minutes, but they made it back to the car. Scott was standing next to the car, waiting. When he saw them, he asked, "Is Mark okay?"

"He's alive," Mike said, "but he is not okay."

"Shit," Scott said. "This is my fault. I talked him into bypassing the blockade."

"We can worry about fault later. We need to get him into the car," Beth said.

Scott opened the back door and helped slide Mark into the back seat. He then picked up Mark's legs and squeezed in next to him.

"Hurry," Scott said as they got on the road. "He risked his life to save me. I can't let anything happen to him."

Beth drove exceedingly fast, and they made it to the hospital in less than twenty minutes. She stopped the car in front of the emergency entrance. Mike looked back and said, "Wait here."

He and Beth got out and raced inside. Without bothering to check in, Mike yelled, "We have an emergency outside. Two victims of an animal attack. One is unconscious." Maybe it was the fact that Mike was wearing his ranger uniform, but in less than a minute, two men were outside with a gurney.

Neither Beth nor Mike wanted to hang around the hospital doing paperwork, so Beth just showed the intake person her FBI identification. As the two men were brought inside, Beth handed her business card to Scott. She said, "Please let me know if your friend will be okay."

***

When they returned to the car, Beth looked at the blood-stained back seat and said, "Well, at least it's vinyl. It should come off." She looked at her white shirt and saw several red spots on it. "This might be a little harder to get clean."

Mike's shirt had even more blood on it. "I don't know if we want to go to a restaurant looking like we just murdered someone."

"I don't care," Beth said. "I'm starving. Besides, it might make for an interesting evening."

Mike smiled and said, "It could be funny in a twisted sort of way. So where should we go?"

"I don't know. I'm hungry. Let's go to the first restaurant we see."

That restaurant happened to be a Mexican restaurant. It was in an eclectic part of town. They passed several gift shops and antique stores before seeing the restaurant. It was a free-standing building painted white with green trim and a red roof. Beth and Mike walked in, and a sign greeted them that said, "Please seat yourself."

They found a table away from other people and sat down. Soon, a young woman came to their table, set menus down in front of them, and said, "Hello. My name is Jennifer. I will be your..." She noticed the blood and had a look of shock on her face. Beth and Mike both looked up when she suddenly stopped talking. She recovered quickly and said, "Oh, wow! Is that blood? Are you two okay?"

"We're okay," Mike said, "but if you see a police car pull into your parking lot, please let us know."

Beth had just opened her menu. She looked up, smiled, and said, "He's kidding," but she didn't elaborate. Let her have her doubts.

The waitress said, "Uh, well, can I get you something to drink?"

"Just water for me, " Beth said.

"Same for me," said Mike.

The waitress walked away, and Beth asked, "Do you think she'll come back?"

"If she does, I think we can expect exceptional service."

They both laughed, and Beth said, "You know, I hope this doesn't sound callous because of all the bad things that have happened, but I am enjoying my time with you."

"That's not callous. You shouldn't let things that happen out of your control dictate your happiness level. I know that you take no pleasure in people getting hurt. Nobody does. Well, almost nobody does. But bad things happen, and we still have to live our lives and try to be happy. I'm enjoying my time with you, too, and I'm not going to feel guilty about it."

"That was a great speech, Mike."

"You think so? I always hated giving speeches in school. I get nervous speaking in front of a group."

The waitress arrived with their drinks and put them on the table. "Are you ready, or do you need more time?" she said.

Beth said, "I'll have an order of the chimichangas."

"I'll have the chicken fajitas," Mike said.

"Very good. Is there anything else I can get you?"

"Yes," Mike said. "I need the biggest knife you have."

Beth slapped him on the arm and said, "Stop! If we frighten our server, she won't come back." She looked at the young woman and said, "We didn't murder anyone. We brought two people to the hospital who were attacked by a wild animal."

The young woman looked relieved and said, "Of course. We get a lot of people in here from the hospital. I just never had any that were bloody."

"Well, now you have a story to tell," Beth said.

When the waitress left, Beth said, "I'm sorry. It was funny, but I didn't want to scare the girl too much."

"That's fine," Mike said. "I probably shouldn't have pushed it. I just felt like having a little fun."

"Well, the fun is over. We should eat quickly when the food comes because I want to get back. I feel like I need a shower now."

"I know what you mean. I need a shower, too."

When they were done eating, Beth drove Mike back to his cabin so he could pick up clean clothes. When he went inside, he could hear noises coming from Dave's room. He stopped to listen and then realized that Dave's girlfriend must have come to see him. She was obviously there to help him feel better.

Mike decided to be quiet and quickly grabbed his clothes. He was about to leave, but thought of something else he might need. He went to the refrigerator and took out a package of bacon and a carton of eggs, which only had four eggs left in it. He put them both in a grocery bag and returned to Beth's car. He said, "Dave is with his girlfriend, so it's a good thing I'm staying with you tonight."

"Wait a minute. Did I say you could spend the night?"

"Well, no, but I thought . . ."

"Relax. I'm joking. Of course, you can stay with me, but there is a condition."

"A condition? What's that?"

"A condition is a requirement, but that's not important right now," Beth said.

"Surely you must be joking," Mike said, and they both laughed.

Beth wanted to say, "Don't call me Shirley," but she was laughing too hard, and the words wouldn't come out.

"Okay," Mike finally said. "What is the condition that you refer to?"

"You must please me," Beth said.

"Please you, huh? Is that possible?"

Beth slapped Mike on the arm, and he said, "Relax. I'm kidding. I accept your challenge. We have all night. I'm sure I could come up with something. Maybe many somethings."

"Oh, multiple pleasings. I can't wait to see what you can do."

Chapter 10

The next morning, Mike cooked the bacon and eggs that he brought from his place. They sat together and ate breakfast before getting ready to start their day. The EPA people would be there by nine, so they had no time to fool around. When they were ready, Mike drove to the visitor's center, where everyone planned on meeting.

Beth's phone rang while they were on the way to the meeting. It was a number with no name. Beth answered and hit the speaker button, "Agent Hartley," she said.

"Agent Hartley. This is Scott. The guy you helped last night. I don't think I thanked you and the ranger properly last night. I really appreciate what you two did for us."

"It was our pleasure to help," Beth said.

"I wanted to let you know that Mark is going to be okay. We won't finish the trail this year, of course, but he wants to come back next year and finish the trail from where we left off."

"Walking the trail in two seasons is still a great accomplishment," Mike said.

"That's what Mark said. I'm just happy he wants to continue."

"How is your ear?" Beth asked.

"It will never look normal again, but that's okay. At least I will have a story to tell."

"Well, we wish both of you the best," Beth said.

They said their goodbyes, and Beth hung up the call just before they arrived at the meeting place. They were ten minutes early, but the EPA people were already there. This time, besides the two vans, they also had a mobile laboratory that looked like a small motor home from the outside. Next to that was an ambulance standing by.

There were more people, too. Eleven people stood in the parking lot while the superintendent went over everything that had happened to date. When Mike and Beth approached, he said, "In case you haven't already met, this is Ranger Mike Bauer and FBI Agent Beth Hartley. They have been investigating the strange happenings around here and know even more than I do about them. If you have any questions, they will be glad to answer them for you. Ranger Mike will be escorting most of you to the crash site, so he will need some protective gear." He looked at Beth and asked, "Will you be going along too, Agent Hartley?"

"I wouldn't miss it, sir," Beth said.

"Very well. Agent Hartley will also need protective gear."

Doctor Catherine Blake, the team leader, approached Beth and Mike. She shook their hands and said, "It's a pleasure to see you two again. How is Ranger David doing today?"

"I don't know about today, but he was doing quite well last night," Mike said.

"That's good to hear. Follow me, and I will get you two set up."

She led them to one of the vans, where several members of her team were standing outside putting on their protective gear. She pulled out a couple of coveralls, gloves, and breathing devices. Mike held up the coveralls and asked, "Is all this really necessary? I mean, wouldn't the oxygen masks be enough?"

"We don't know what we are dealing with yet," she said. "The indications are that whatever it is out there is airborne, but it is also possible that it could be absorbed through the skin. We just don't know yet. Do you want to take that chance?"

"No, I guess not," Mike said.

"I understand that all this stuff is uncomfortable," said Doctor Blake, "but you will get used to it."

After everyone finished getting dressed, Mike went to his vehicle and removed his tranquilizer pistol from the back. The coveralls had two pockets, so he put the tranquilizer gun in one pocket and his radio and cell phone in the other. He also wanted to bring a small box of extra darts, but had nowhere to put it, so he asked Beth to carry it for him. He thought about bringing the rifle, but decided he didn't want to carry it. He knew Beth was armed, so he figured he wouldn't need it.

Mike, Beth, Doctor Blake, and seven members of her team got in the two vans and drove as close as they could to the part of the trail they needed to go to. The ambulance followed and parked behind them. They carried their facemasks with them until they reached the place where they had to leave the trail and walk into the woods. Unlike the day before, the weather was beautiful. The sun was shining, and the temperature was low enough to make the extra clothing almost bearable.

Having been through this part of the woods twice before, Doctor Blake and her team were more familiar with where they were going than Mike. Mike knew he was more of a protector than a guide, so he was content to let Doctor Blake take the lead. As they walked, Mike kept his hand on his tranquilizer gun while he scanned the area for potential threats. He even occasionally stopped to look behind them to make sure they weren't being stalked, even though he knew animals pumped up with adrenaline would not be interested in quietly stalking their prey.

"Doctor Blake, what will happen after you find the cause of all these problems?" Beth asked. "I mean, how long will it take to get this place back to normal?"

"That's a tough question to answer without knowing what the problem is. It could be anywhere from a couple of days to several years. Some contaminated sites just can't be safely cleaned up. We end up closing them off indefinitely."

Beth shook her head and said, "I sure hope that doesn't happen here."

"I agree," said Doctor Blake. "It is a beautiful area. I would hate to lose it."

When they got close, Doctor Blake pointed at the broken treetops and said, "We're getting close. That's where the meteorite came down."

They picked up their pace a little, but slogging through the woods without a clear trail was still slow going. When they reached the clearing where the meteorite had hit, the size of the crater left behind by the meteorite surprised Beth and Mike. "Wow! No wonder people thought we had an earthquake," Mike said.

"So, if the meteorite wasn't toxic, do you think it disturbed something under the ground here?" Beth asked. "Maybe there is some kind of gas pocket under there."

"It's possible," said Doctor Blake. "That's what we're here to find out."

She turned to the rest of her crew and said, Okay, you all know what to do. I need air and soil samples from the crater and all around this area. Make sure you mark every spot where you take the sample."

The people got to work taking air samples, digging up dirt, and placing it in glass containers. They then placed markers in the spots where the dirt came from and wrote the marker numbers on the labels. Once all the samples were collected and packed away, someone photographed the entire area.

When they finished, they headed back. Mike led the way, this time with Beth right behind him. When they returned, Doctor Blake's team brought the samples directly to their mobile lab and began analyzing them immediately.

Beth and Mike waited outside for a few minutes until Doctor Blake came out and said, "We probably won't know anything for at least two hours. It's almost noon. Why don't you two go have lunch? Come back around two. We should know something by then."

Beth and Mike looked at each other, and Beth said, "Well, I am getting hungry."

"Me too," Mike said. "Let's go back to my place. There might be food there if Dave hasn't eaten it all."

***

They headed back to Mike's cabin. When they arrived, they found Dave sitting on the sofa watching television. He still had a bandage on his face, but he looked well otherwise. He turned the television off and said, "Hey, you two. How was your foray into the woods this morning?"

"Unlike yours, it was uneventful," Mike said. "The science geeks got their samples, and we are just waiting for the results. Where's Patty? I thought she came to be with you."

"She had to work this morning. She'll be back later."

"We just came for lunch. Did you eat yet?"

"Not yet, Buddy. Are you making lunch?"

"I guess I am," Mike said, "if there is anything left to make."

"Don't worry about that. Patty brought us some groceries. She brought bread and some lunchmeat if you feel like a sandwich."

Mike saw a bag of small hoagie rolls on the counter, along with a head of lettuce and a couple of tomatoes. He opened the refrigerator and found a package of roast beef. He looked at Beth and asked, "Are you up for a roast beef sandwich?"

"Of course," Beth said. "That sounds good."

While Mike prepared the sandwiches, Beth sat on a chair beside the sofa and said, "So, how are you feeling today, Dave?"

"I feel fine. I'm ready to go back to work. This forced time off is boring."

"I can imagine. Do you know when you will be able to return to work?"

"I have an appointment to see the doctor the day after tomorrow. Hopefully, I'll get the green light then."

"I'm sure you can handle two more days of relaxing."

Mike finished the sandwiches and put them on the table. "Lunch is served," he said.

"You mean you're not going to bring them to us?" Dave asked."

"Keep dreaming, Buddy."

Dave looked at Beth and said, "I always thought injured people got pampered. If I had known, I would have avoided that crazed animal."

"Well, now you know for next time," Beth said.

They got up and joined Mike at the table. Beth took a bite of her sandwich and said, "This is good. Thanks, Mike."

"We should be thanking Dave's girlfriend. Without her, we'd be eating canned soup and potato chips."

"I'd be happy with that, too," Beth said.

"Really?" Mike asked.

"Don't be so surprised. You should know I'm not a prima donna by now."

"No, you certainly are not that. I bet you could survive alone on a deserted island. It's a bit of a turn-on."

"Okay, you two, get a room," Dave said.

"I'd like to, but we're on the clock," Mike said.

"Speaking of that, when will they know something?" Dave asked.

Mike looked at his watch and said, "We should know something in about an hour. They brought a mobile lab with them this time."

"What are you going to do if they don't find anything?"

"What are you talking about? They took samples from the entire area. They have to find something."

Beth shook her head and said, "I hope they figure this out, but I'm not going to hold my breath on this one this time."

Mike looked at her, surprised at her pessimism. "Really? Do you think something else is going on around here? Do you still think it is some terrorist testing ground?"

"I don't know what to think. I know we were disappointed before, so I'm hoping for the best but planning for the worst."

"So, what if the worst happens? What if they find nothing?"

"Then we just keep plugging along. We have protective gear now. If we have to, we will just get back out there until we find the culprit."

"Now, I'm eager to put this to rest. Let's go back and see if they learned anything yet."

"But I'm not done with my sandwich yet."

"Bring it with you," Mike said as he headed toward the door.

Beth took another bite and put the rest of the sandwich on her plate. She put her hand on Dave's shoulder. "Sorry," she said as she raced to catch up to Mike.

***

They both got in Mike's vehicle, and Beth said, "What's the hurry?"

"I'm sorry, Beth. I just need to know. If we have to go out searching again, I want to do it while we still have plenty of daylight."

When they returned to the visitor's center, they saw several people hanging out near the mobile lab. They had split into small groups and were talking amongst themselves. Some had drinks in their hands. They didn't see Doctor Blake, so Mike knocked on the door. Doctor Blake opened it and peered outside. "Oh, Agent Hartley. Ranger Mike. You're back early."

"Have you learned anything yet?" Mike asked.

"I'm afraid not," she said. "We haven't tested all the samples yet, but everything we have tested so far came up negative for harmful chemicals. I don't hold out much hope that the remaining samples will be any different, but you never know."

"Okay. Thank you, Doctor. We'll check back in a little bit."

Mike held out his hand and said, "Come on."

Beth took his hand, and he led her toward the building. "Where are we going?"

"Just inside. I'll show you."

Inside, there was an information desk as well as several shelves with merchandise on them. Mike found a map of the park and picked it up. He spread the map out on the counter and said, "I need a pen."

Beth looked around and found a basket full of pens. She handed one to Mike. He studied the map carefully and said, "Okay, here is where the meteorite hit." He drew a small circle and filled it in. He drew two more small circles and said, "This is where the bear attacked that man, and this is where Dave was attacked."

He thought a little more and drew another circle. "I think this is where the two men we found were injured, but I didn't think to get a GPS reading."

Beth looked at the map and asked, "Where was Emma Drake's campsite?"

Mike thought for a moment and circled it with his pen, "They camped right here."

"So, draw a line from the campsite to the meteorite. Whatever is out there should fall along that line."

"Good idea," Mike said and drew a line.

"That's still a fairly big area. Whatever we are looking for is not going to stand out like a neon sign."

"The ducks," Mike said, and got out his phone. He found the GPS coordinates from the screenshot he had saved and entered them into his map software. He looked at the display and compared it to his paper map. "We found the ducks here," he said and drew a circle. He then drew a line heading south-southeast until it crossed the first line he drew.

Beth looked at the intersection and picked up the pen. She drew a circle around all the incident points. The intersection fell almost in the middle of the circle. "It looks like we found a new place to search."

Mike folded the map and said, "Come on. We need to take advantage of the daylight we have left."

They went back to the mobile lab and knocked on the door. Doctor Blake answered again and said, "I'm afraid that entire area is free of contaminants. We found nothing more than trace amounts of a few different chemicals, but nothing even close to a toxic level."

"That's because we were looking in the wrong area," Beth said.

She looked at Mike, who nodded and unfolded his map. He pointed his finger at a spot on the map and said, "This is where the meteorite was." He moved his finger slightly up and to the left. "This is where we need to search. It's a little more than a quarter mile northwest of the original location."

She looked at Mike and then at Beth and asked, "Are you sure about this?"

Beth shrugged, and Mike said, "We can't be sure about anything, but we considered where all the incidents took place, and this makes the most sense."

Doctor Blake thought for a moment and finally said, "Okay. I'll get my team."

"No," Mike said. "Just you. We may not find anything, and I don't want to be responsible for the safety of so many people if it is not necessary."

"Very well," Doctor Blake said before calling her team together. She told them she would be going without them to check something out, and they should wait for further instructions.

Chapter 11

They all put their protective gear back on, but before heading back into the woods, Mike figured out the GPS coordinates of their destination and entered them into his phone. Since there was no road to take to their destination, the map software was confused, so Mike turned off the volume and focused on the map.

Mike again carried his tranquilizer pistol in his pocket and scanned the forest carefully as they trudged through the woods. They eventually reached the area with few trees, and Beth said, "I remember seeing this earlier today, but we passed in a different spot."

"Yes. We were a bit south of here."

"Why are there no tall trees along this narrow strip?"

"That's interesting," Doctor Blake said. "I saw this too, but just considered it a fluke of nature. I hadn't noticed how straight and how far it went. Did something kill the trees years ago?"

"Lumberjacks, I imagine," Mike said. "I heard a road ran through here a long time ago. It was probably put here before this place was a national park. That would have been ninety years ago or more." He pointed to a small white patch. "Look. You can still see small patches of gravel."

I'm surprised Mother Nature hasn't completely covered it over," Beth said.

"Mother Nature never fails to surprise me," Mike said. "She is almost as good at tearing things down as she is at building them up."

He looked at the map on his phone and said, "We are getting close. We just need to follow this old road north for a few hundred feet."

They continued down the old road until they reached the end. The tall trees resumed in front of them. Mike looked at the map on his phone and said, "We're here."

They all looked around, and Doctor Blake said, "Everything looks normal. I don't know what we are looking for."

Beth said, "Don't you find it a bit strange that this ninety-year-old road ends exactly where we predicted the source of our problems would be?"

"Do you think this old road is related to our new problem?" Mike asked.

"I don't know," Beth said. "It could be related, but I have no idea how."

"I think I might know," Doctor Blake said. When that meteorite hit, it created a strong tremor that some people mistook for an earthquake. What if someone used this road to dispose of chemicals? They might have buried them underground around here. Maybe that waste was in barrels that burst open when the tremor hit."

"That makes a lot of sense," Beth said. "Do you have any idea where we should look?"

"I have an idea," Mike said. "If the road stopped here, then this is where they must have buried the chemicals if that is what they were doing. They wouldn't bury anything under the road, but it probably wouldn't be more than a hundred feet or so from the road. So I would guess we will find what we are looking for within a hundred-foot radius from where we are standing." He looked around and said, "The woods are less dense to the east. Let's look that way first."

They spread out with Beth to the right and Doctor Blake to the left. A large oak tree stood in front of Mike. A large branch from the tree lay on the ground to the left. When Mike got close, he said, "Look at this. This branch fell off recently."

They met up by the tree. Doctor Blake said, "The tremor from the meteorite must have caused it to break loose."

Mike looked around. About a hundred feet beyond the tree was a small stream, but he saw nothing out of the ordinary.

Beth made her way to the other side of the fallen branch and said, "You're not going to believe this."

Mike and Doctor Blake rushed over to where Beth was standing and looked down in surprise at what they saw. A pair of doors lay on the ground next to the fallen branch, like the entrance to a storm cellar, but in the middle of nowhere. "What the hell?" Mike said.

"Exactly," Beth said. "I think we will find what we are looking for down there."

The metal doors were rusty with several small holes in them. One hole was big enough to put a fist through. A padlock held the two doors together, but it was quite rusty, too. Mike grabbed one of the handles and pulled hard, but the handle broke instead of the lock. He tried again with the other handle, but instead of one strong pull, he rattled the door up and down until the hinge holding the padlock snapped off.

Mike pulled both doors open, and they all looked inside. They could see stairs leading down into a dark room. They all took out their phones and turned on the flashlights. "Wait here. I'll check it out," Mike said and started down the stairs.

"Wait here, my ass," Beth said and followed him down the stairs with Doctor Blake close behind.

The bottom of the stairway opened to what looked like a crude office. There was a metal desk to the left with a black and white photograph of Herbert Hoover hanging behind it on the wall. To the right stood several file cabinets lined up along the wall. On the opposite wall, past the file cabinets, was a door.

On top of the desk sat two metal trays, which Mike assumed were an inbox and an outbox. One of the boxes still contained papers. Mike picked up the top paper. It was very yellow and dusty, but still readable. "This is dated March 10, 1933," Mike said. "It's from the Office of the President of The United States ordering this place to be closed down." He thought about it and said, "That was right after Roosevelt took office."

"So this must have been some kind of government facility," Beth said. "What the hell were they doing out here in the middle of nowhere?"

Doctor Blake, who had been thumbing through one of the file cabinets, spoke up, "Research. This entire file cabinet contains information about something called "Batch 9.""

"Batch 9? So they were developing some kind of chemical?" Beth asked.

"It would seem so, Doctor Blake said as she read one of the files. "It will take weeks to go through all these documents, but from what I have seen so far, it looks like they were developing chemical weapons."

"I thought they outlawed chemical weapons after the First World War," Mike said.

"Not until 1925," Doctor Blake said. "Some of these files date back to 1922. If I keep looking, I might find some earlier than that."

"Why wasn't this place closed in 1925 then?" Mike asked.

"Really, Mike? You need to ask that?" Beth asked.

"What was I thinking?"

"I think we need to see what's behind door number one," Beth said.

"Agreed," Mike said before opening the door.

They all pointed their lights into the room before going inside. Straight ahead and to the left were two large tables, perhaps twelve feet long and five feet wide. Each table contained dozens of glass beakers and hoses, along with various other scientific components. A microscope stood on the end of each of the tables. At the far left was a large sink. Next to the sink were wooden shelves with various pieces of scientific equipment. The back wall contained dozens of empty cages. To the right, along the wall, were several shelving units, all holding various-sized glass containers.

The two bottom shelves near the door had collapsed, and all the bottles were broken. The floor was wet with a thick, milky liquid. Some of it had seeped under the door. "Watch where you step," Mike said. "You don't want to get that stuff on your shoes."

They all entered the room, stepping over the liquid. They shone their lights on the broken bottles and the shelves above them. "These are all labeled 'Batch 9," Doctor Blake said. "We need to learn what this stuff is."

They all stepped over the liquid and went back into the office. Doctor Blake pulled a handful of files and handed them to Beth. She gave another stack to Mike. "We need to look through these and figure out what the hell batch 9 is."

Beth set her papers on the desk and sat in the chair. She held the light with her left hand while flipping through the papers with her right. Mike placed his files on the other side of the desk and looked through them while Doctor Blake stood at the file cabinet, looking through documents.

"Here's a paper dated September 3, 1932," Mike said. "It reads, 'Preliminary testing indicates that Batch 9 has fallen short of expectations, especially in the non-lethal requirement. So far, seven out of ten test rats have died after first becoming extremely aggressive.' It looks like they were trying to develop a non-lethal weapon."

"They obviously failed," Beth said. "I have a report here that is dated September 29, 1932. It says, 'The formula, Batch 9, was administered to five monkeys at fifty percent toxicity. All five exhibited aggressive behavior, followed by the death of four of the five monkeys.'"

"That makes it seem even more toxic at a lower dose," Mike said.

"It's hard to make a judgment from just two tests," Doctor Blake said. We don't know how healthy the animals were to begin with. It could also be that rats are more resilient to that chemical than monkeys are. So anyway, what has been happening around here is very clear. The tremor, or the falling tree branch, caused those shelves to collapse, spilling a dangerous chemical on the floor. Batch 9 starts in liquid form, but it is designed to be used as a gas. As it evaporates, a hazardous chemical enters the air and seeps out through the gaps in the door. Any person or animal who walked by this area would be affected."

Doctor Blake pulled out another paper and read it. She said, "This is dated December 18, 1932. It basically says that Batch 9 had the opposite effect as intended. Instead of making the subjects fearful so they would retreat, it made them aggressive so they would attack. I can see why that would not be very helpful in a war."

Why would they just leave all this stuff here?" Mike asked. "It seems very irresponsible."

"It sure does," Doctor Blake said. "If I were to guess, I would say cleaning it up was a low priority to them at the time. I'm sure they planned to send a cleanup crew, but the paperwork probably got lost, and this place was essentially forgotten."

"So what's the next step?" Mike asked.

"The next step is to get a cleanup crew out here as soon as possible. Considering the delicate nature of moving this stuff, it will probably take weeks to remove everything, but I think once we block off this area and clean the spill, we can reopen this section of the park. Two days, maybe. Three tops."

"That's good news. It will be nice to get back to normal," Mike said. He noticed Beth had a somewhat disappointed look on her face and added, "Although I will miss having a partner."

Beth smiled and said, "You won't know what to do without me."

"You may be right about that. Right now, we should get out of here so we can report our findings."

Mike led the way up the stairs. When they were all standing on the ground outside, Mike closed one door, and

Beth closed the other. Mike stood looking at the door for a moment and asked, "Is there anything we can cover this door with to keep the gas from escaping?"

"There's plastic in one of the vans, but nothing here," Doctor Blake said.

Beth turned to see what might be in nature that they could use and saw something that made her scream. Mike turned and saw a large black bear ten yards away and moving towards them. He pulled Beth backward and stepped in front of her. The bear stopped five feet away, stood tall on its hind legs, and growled.

Mike, seeing an opportunity, pulled out his tranquilizer gun and fired point-blank into the bear's chest. It dropped to all fours and growled even louder. Mike turned to the two women and yelled, "Run!"

He turned back to face the bear as it knocked him off his feet. The bear was on top of him as it swung at Mike's face with its powerful claws. His mask flew off, and the bear let out a massive growl into his face. He could smell the bear's breath and knew this was the end for him. He only hoped he distracted the bear long enough for Beth and Doctor Blake to escape.

Just then, a stick hit the bear on its head. Mike couldn't see where the stick came from, but noticed that the bear's attention had turned away. The stick hit the bear again. Mike turned his head and saw Beth beating the bear with a tree branch. "Beth! Get out of here!" Mike yelled, but she kept hitting the bear until it started chasing her.

Beth threw the branch at the bear, took out her gun, and ran. The bear chased her quickly at first, but its speed gradually diminished until it could no longer run or even walk, for that matter. Beth stopped and turned. She pointed the gun at the bear as it lay on the ground and fell asleep. She stood there, watching it breathe for several seconds, then put her gun away and raced back to Mike.

Doctor Blake was already at his side, helping him to his feet. When Beth got close, she said, "Help me. We have to get him away from here quickly. Hopefully, it's not too late."

Beth picked up the dart gun and put it in her pocket. She got on the other side of Mike and put his arm around her shoulders. His chest and arms were bloody, but his face mask protected his face from the bear's claws. "I should probably tell you that as much as I like two lovely ladies paying attention to me simultaneously, I can walk just fine," Mike said.

"Okay, tough guy. Let's see what you got," Beth said.

Mike started walking, and Beth and Doctor Blake followed. He picked up his pace, and the two women raced to keep up with him. "Slow down!" Doctor Blake yelled. "You need to keep your heart rate down."

Mike stopped and turned around. He felt his chest. "Oh, my God. I inhaled that stuff. My heart is racing. Shit! I don't want to die out here. We need to get back before it's too late."

Mike turned around and started running, but a dart hit him on the back of his right shoulder. He stopped and reached around with his left hand and removed it. He looked back and saw Beth holding the tranquilizer gun. "You shot me. Why?"

Beth caught up to him, put her arm around him, and said, "Because I've grown attached to you, and I don't want you to die."

Doctor Blake got on the other side of Mike, and the two helped him walk. They made it halfway back to the trail when Mike became too tired to continue. They set him down, and Beth used his radio and reported that a bear had attacked Mike, and they were bringing him in. She said he was exposed to the toxin and needed the paramedics to meet them on the trail. They picked him up again and struggled to carry him through the woods. Two paramedics and several rangers were waiting on the trail. As soon as they saw them, they quickly made their way through the woods and carried Mike the rest of the way. Once they were on the trail, they put him on a stretcher and carried him to the waiting ambulance.

Beth got in the back of the ambulance with Mike, and they left for the hospital. "He was exposed to the chemical," Beth said to the paramedic.

"Yes. We were briefed on that," he said. "I just don't understand why his heart rate is normal, even a little below normal. We were expecting him to be on the verge of a heart attack."

"I shot him with a tranquilizer dart," Beth said.

The paramedic looked surprised and said, "That was smart thinking. You probably saved his life."

Chapter 12

As Beth waited in the hospital's waiting room for word on Mike's condition, several people from the park showed up. Dave arrived first with his girlfriend. A few minutes later, Superintendent Johnson came with four of his rangers. They waited for what seemed an eternity, but it was really about thirty minutes. Finally, a doctor came out to brief them. She said, "I am confident that Ranger Bauer will make a full recovery."

Everyone hugged each other when they heard the news. The doctor waited for the commotion to die down, turned to Beth, and asked, "Are you the one who tranquilized him?"

"That would be me," Beth said.

"You saved his life," she said.

"He saved mine first," Beth replied.

"The doctor put her hand on Beth's shoulder and said, "He'll be okay. We will keep him sedated until the chemicals are out of his system. Go home and get some rest. Come back tomorrow afternoon."

"Thank you, Doctor," Beth said before the doctor walked away.

Dave approached Beth and asked, "Are you okay?"

"Yes, I'm fine," Beth said, wiping a tear from her eye.

"Would you like a ride back to your cabin?"

"That would be great. Thank you, Dave."

When Beth returned to her cabin, she took out the business card from Senator Drake. She opened her laptop and sent him an email. She then got busy. She had a lot of searching to do.

***

Beth woke up late the following morning. She was usually an early bird, but she had been up later than usual the night before. She made herself a cup of coffee and then checked her email. She received a reply from Senator Drake. She also had replies from other inquiries she had made the previous evening.

After getting ready, she headed into town. She didn't go to the hospital to see Mike right away. She had too much to do. By three o'clock, she had accomplished everything she had set out to do and headed to the hospital.

At the nurses' station, she said she was there to see Mike Bauer. One of the nurses said, "He's in room 312. I believe he is still sedated, but you can go in to see him. On the way to the room, Beth saw the doctor from the day before and asked, "How is Mike doing?"

The doctor thought for a moment and then said, "Oh, the ranger. We stopped his medication about an hour ago. He should be waking up soon. I'm sure he would love to see a familiar face when he does wake up."

"Thank you so much, Doctor," Beth said and headed to room 312. She found Mike sleeping, pulled a chair next to the bed, and sat down. She slipped her hand under his and put her other hand on top. Mike's eyes slowly fluttered open.

"I must be dead," he said. "I see an angel."

Beth smiled and said, "You are quite the smooth talker. It seems the student has become the master."

"Don't let Dave hear you say that."

"He's a good friend," Beth said. "He was here last night, along with Superintendent Johnson and a few fellow rangers. You have a lot of friends."

"Yes, friends who wouldn't shoot me. You shot me."

"Don't be a baby. I saved your life."

"How did you know that would work?"

"I saw the bear sleeping peacefully. It occurred to me that the tranquilizer counteracted the poison. I know it was risky, but it was the only thing I could think of at the time."

"You made the right choice, and it took a lot of balls to beat on that bear the way you did," Mike said. "I don't know whether to admire you or fear you."

Beth patted Mike on the cheek and said, "You should do both."

"You had your gun. You could have shot the bear. Why didn't you?"

"The truth is, when I saw that bear, I froze. All my training went out the window. You pulled me back and saved me. When I regained my senses, I partly feared that the gun would just piss him off more."

"More than beating him on the head with a stick?"

"Well, I guess mostly I felt bad for the bear. None of this was the bear's fault."

"You have a good heart, Beth. By the way, have you heard any news about the chemical cleanup?"

"There are people out there right now taking care of it. They expect to have the park open the day after tomorrow. Of course, they will still be getting everything out of there for quite a while, but life must go on, as they say."

"I'm glad we were able to figure out what was going on around here. I'm guessing this means you will be leaving now."

"Are you in a hurry to get rid of me?"

"No. Not at all. Quite the opposite. I was getting used to having you around."

"How would you feel if I stayed around here longer?"

"Really? How much longer?"

"Oh, I don't know. I was thinking indefinitely."

Mike looked surprised and said, "Are you serious?"

"I have to go back to Washington for a couple of weeks, but then I'll start my new job with the local sheriff's department here. I even secured an apartment in town."

"That's awesome. How in the world did you get a job in one day?"

"Well, it helps to know a certain senator who can write a letter of recommendation and maybe pull a few strings."

"It seems like a bit of a demotion after being with the FBI. Are you sure this is what you want?"

"Someone very wise told me recently that the goal of life should be to be happy. I believe that I am finally on the right path to accomplish that goal."

"I guess that same someone pushed you off that fence you were sitting on."

Beth took Mike's Hand and squeezed. "I was lucky to meet such a wise man," Beth said. "Perhaps I will introduce you someday."

"Very funny," Mike said.

"That same person also told me I should love someone."

"Really. So are you going to take his advice?"

"I already have," Beth said before leaning in to kiss Mike. She pulled away and said, "In spite of my best efforts to resist, you somehow made me fall in love with you, Michael Bauer. I think I knew it when that bear was on top of you. The thought that I might lose you frightened me more than anything I could remember."

Mike squeezed Beth's hand and said, "I love you, too, Bethany Hartley. You have proven to be a partner I can count on. When I thought I was going to die, I took comfort in knowing you had a chance to get away. When you started beating on that bear, the fear returned, but at the same time, I felt proud to have such a wonderful partner who would risk her life for me."

"You did the same for me. I guess we make a good team."

They kissed again, and Mike said, "I have little doubt you will work your way up to sheriff one day soon."

"I appreciate the confidence, but my ambitions have changed. I think I want to settle down, get married, and have a couple of kids. Do you like kids, Mike?"

"I would love to have kids. Wait a minute. Did you just ask me to marry you?"

Beth paused for a moment and said, "I believe I did. Yes. Mike, will you marry me?"

"Of course, I will marry you, but I have a condition."

"A condition? What is it? Beth asked and laughed.

"Mike laughed too and said, "Don't get me started, Shirley."

They both laughed and then kissed again. Beth smiled and said, "Okay, what is your condition?"

"My condition is that you need to make the coffee.

I truly appreciate you taking the time to read Falling Star. I hope you enjoyed the story.

I would be incredibly grateful if you left a review on Amazon, Goodreads, or wherever you purchased this book. Your thoughts help other readers discover my books and mean a lot to me as an author. Whether it's a few words or a detailed review, your feedback makes a difference.

Thank you again for your support. I couldn't do this without readers like you.

Charles Huss

Books by Charles Huss

Last Healer Mysteries Series

Joe, a reclusive, ageless centenarian, meets Katie, an ambitious news personality with dreams of being an investigative reporter. Together, they solve crimes and explore the full potential of Joe's healing abilities while navigating the complexities of their intimate relationship.

The Last Healer

On the eve of her thirtieth birthday, Katie, a television news reporter, unhappy with her career and her love life, decides to spend the weekend alone at a Wisconsin ski resort.

Joe is a man content to live a private life in his cabin in the woods. Since the death of his wife, he has avoided intimate relationships and prefers to keep a low profile to prevent people from learning of his unusual abilities.

On the way to the ski resort, Katie makes a wrong turn during a snowstorm and hits Joe with her car. Lost and with no cell signal, Katie tries to keep Joe alive until she can get help. During Joe's recovery, Katie learns his secret and soon helps to investigate his family's mysterious past while Joe helps Katie investigate a double murder. Love blossoms while they slowly unravel both mysteries, but danger lies ahead. Can Joe discover the full extent of his abilities before it is too late?

Book Two - Last Rites

In this gripping sequel to "The Last Healer," Katie and Joe, fresh from their honeymoon, must race to Milwaukee to save the life of Katie's dear friend Ashley after she and her mother fall victim to a ruthless attack. With Ashley on the brink of death, while a priest delivers Last Rites, her only chance for survival is Joe's remarkable healing powers.

What starts as a rescue mission turns into a murder investigation as they investigate the killing of Ashley's mother. While searching for the shooter, their investigation leads them to a chilling conspiracy centered on the city's homeless population. As they uncover more of the truth, they become targets as someone is determined to silence them. Will Katie and Joe find who is behind a series of murders, or will they become the next victims?

Last Chance

In Book Three of the Last Healer Mysteries, Katie and Joe, after deciding to quit investigating murders, are thrust back into it when a man is murdered at Joe's resort.

The victim is no ordinary man. He is a suspected jewel thief, believed to have hidden stolen jewels at the resort. While they struggle to handle all the treasure seekers, Katie and Joe debate how involved they should be in the murder investigation. They don't know the killer lurks in the background, taking orders from some of the most powerful people in Wisconsin while he waits for Katie and Joe to find what he is looking for.

Last Flight

In Book Four of the Last Healer Mysteries series, Katie and Joe witness the deadly crash of a prototype aircraft and save the life of one of its occupants. After Joe discovers evidence of sabotage, Katie insists she can investigate the crime despite being almost nine months pregnant.

Someone planted an explosive device in the aircraft, killing the company's founder and jeopardizing the struggling startup's future. Was the attack meant to destroy the company, or was it something more personal? As Katie and Joe hit one dead end after another, they discover the killer isn't finished. With time running out, they race to save the next victim, but with people dying, a murderer on the loose, and Katie in labor, what's a Healer to do?

Last Hope

In the fifth Last Healer Mystery, Katie and Joe learn of a tragedy in Katie's hometown while they are celebrating their son's first birthday. The husband of Katie's childhood best friend stands accused of murdering the community's lone police detective. They return to the small Wisconsin town, determined to find the real killer.

As they dig deeper, they uncover chilling ties between the detective's death and the recent killing of the mayor's daughter. It soon becomes clear someone will stop at nothing to keep the truth buried.

Other Books by Charles Huss

Truth Be Told

Peter Beckett awoke 25 years ago with no memory of his past. Since then, he's been haunted by a gift he never asked for and doesn't want. People can't lie to him. To Peter, it feels like a curse that has left him isolated and feared by all who get to know him. Only his priest accepts him for who he is.

The FBI has been watching him, and they need his unique talent to track a deadly drug cartel that has infiltrated Milwaukee, fueling a dangerous spike of fentanyl overdoses. Rookie agent Hannah Meyers is assigned to recruit Peter, who is reluctant to help, but is intrigued by Hannah after she lies to him.

As the investigation deepens, details of Peter's former life emerge. With secrets unraveling and lives on the line, Peter must decide whether to return to the glorious life he once knew or give it all up for love.

Saving Apollo

Apollo is no ordinary dog. Along with his sister, Athena, he was genetically modified to be smarter than a chimpanzee. When the lead geneticist quits over a dispute about the fate of the dogs, chaos erupts, and Apollo escapes, ending up on a small island off the Florida coast. There, he befriends twelve-year-old Ethan, who has just moved to the island with his dad, Ryan.

As they uncover Apollo's extraordinary ability to understand them, they also learn about the perilous fate that awaits him if he returns. With the help of their neighbor, Brooke, a local veterinarian, they devise a plan to save Apollo and Athena. Standing in their way is Jack Strauss, a former Marine and head of security at the lab that created Apollo and Athena.

"Saving Apollo" is a heartwarming, family-friendly story of friendship, love, and compassion.

Identity Crisis

After Alex Neumann agrees to participate in his father's groundbreaking memory recording experiment, he awakens years later to find he is not the man he used to be. He soon becomes a pawn in a deadly scheme involving a ruthless businessman, an Army general, and the President of The United States.

As Alex peels away layers of deception, his true identity slowly emerges, along with skills foreign to his old self. He will need all those skills and the help of friends he meets along the way to survive and turn the tables on his adversaries.

Bad Cat Chris: The Baddest Cat You'll Ever Love

When Chuck volunteered to help a local cat shelter clean cages one morning, the last thing he expected was a kitten climbing up his back to perch on his shoulders, but that was the beginning of a relationship that would test the limits of human endurance and compassion.

This is the story of Chris, a cat like no other who would turn the lives of Chuck and Rose upside-down while eventually showing them that bad can be good and love can come from the most unlikely places.

This book is based on Chris's blog at BadCatChris.com and is a collection of sometimes serious but mostly humorous stories about the ups and downs of living with a bad cat.

About The Author

Charles Huss was born and raised in the suburbs of Chicago but has lived most of his adult life in the Tampa Bay, Florida, area. He is a St. Petersburg College graduate and the author of several books. He currently lives with his wife, Rose, and their two cats.

Don't miss out!

Visit the website below and you can sign up to receive emails whenever Charles Huss publishes a new book. There's no charge and no obligation.

https://books2read.com/r/B-A-LHRY-SDCHD

BOOKS 2 READ

Connecting independent readers to independent writers.

Did you love *Falling Star*? Then you should read *The Last Healer*[1] by Charles Huss!

[2]

On the eve of her thirtieth birthday, Katie, a television news reporter, unhappy with her career and her love life, decides to spend the weekend alone at a Wisconsin ski resort.

Joe is a man content to live a private life in his cabin in the woods. Since the death of his wife, he has avoided intimate relationships and prefers to keep a low profile to prevent people from learning of his unusual abilities.

On the way to the ski resort, Katie makes a wrong turn during a snowstorm and hits Joe with her car. Lost and with no

1. https://books2read.com/u/3yQJ0B

2. https://books2read.com/u/3yQJ0B

cell signal, Katie tries to keep Joe alive until she can get help. During Joe's recovery, Katie learns his secret and soon helps to investigate his family's mysterious past while Joe helps Katie investigate a double murder. Love blossoms while they slowly unravel both mysteries, but danger lies ahead. Can Joe discover the full extent of his abilities before it is too late?

The Last Healer is part mystery, part romance, and part science fiction. It is a book that can be enjoyed in just a few hours but remembered for a lifetime.

Read more at charleshuss.com.

About the Author

Charles Huss was born and raised in the suburbs of Chicago but has lived most of his adult life in the Tampa Bay, Florida area. He is a graduate of St. Petersburg College and is the author of several books. He currently lives with his wife, Rose, and their two cats.

Read more at charleshuss.com.